MY FATHER'S
GIRLFRIEND

~

MY FATHER'S GIRLFRIEND

Mac-Jane Chukwu

authorHOUSE®

AuthorHouse™
1663 Liberty Drive
Bloomington, IN 47403
www.authorhouse.com
Phone: 1 (800) 839-8640

Published by AuthorHouse 02/11/2015

ISBN: 978-1-4969-6638-4 (sc)
ISBN: 978-1-4969-6686-5 (e)

Library of Congress Control Number: 2015901651

Print information available on the last page.

Foreword

The issues facing women around the globe are of universal concern. Women from all nations and of all faiths and races face challenges daily that expose them to societal ills ranging from fighting cancer to dealing with domestic violence. Although many admirable organizations advocate campaigns that attempt to empower women, uphold women's rights, and encourage human rights and education, their efforts only scratch the surface. In *My Father's Girlfriend*, author Mac-Jane Chukwu explores the darkest challenges that women can face: betrayal, rape, homelessness, and domestic violence. Although *My Father's Girlfriend* is a work of fiction, it is based on events that have been well documented in the global news media. The focal character is a young woman from Nigeria who struggles to make a living and carve a niche for herself in society in the face of overwhelming obstacles.

As the mother of two daughters, I cannot read accounts of abuse against women without thinking of my own children and saying a prayer of thanks that they have been spared such a horrible fate. My older daughter, a former U.S. Air Force officer, now teaches at the university level, while my younger daughter is an assistant attorney general specializing in prosecuting crimes of abuse against children. Each in her own way contributes to the fight against abuse, ignorance, and neglect. Mac-Jane's novel is a multi-faceted work, but at its heart *My Father's Girlfriend* presents a universal challenge to us all: What is our role in this struggle? What contribution are we willing to make?

Evangelist Joyce Meyer, who is a victim of abuse, put it well—and quite simply—when she said, "Is there any real purpose in being alive if all we are going to do is get up every day and live only for ourselves?" Live your life to help others." *My Father's Girlfriend* is heartfelt and reflects not only the literary skill of the author, but also her compassion. I am proud of this young Troy University alumna—and current TROY graduate student—who is using her God-given talent to help others. *My Father's Girlfriend* is a call to action. May this book inspire us to answer this call.

Janice Hawkins,
First Lady of Troy University
January 2015

Dedication

This book is dedicated to the men in my life.

To my father, Maurison Chukwu for being my dad in every sense of the word, for teaching me life principles that really matter. I still remain daddy's girl.

To my only brother, Prince Chukwu; for always making me laugh.

To Marrell Crayton; for the future God has for us.

Acknowledgement

I am thankful for the great support I have as a young woman with huge dreams. I thank God for placing supportive people in my life, those who saw greatness even when I did not. I thank God for inspiration daily and the strength to write-- I do not take it for granted.

I am thankful for my family who painstakingly have to listen to me rave on and on about my writings, they practically have to endure (sometimes) me reading a portion of my stories to them, especially my siblings who listened and would often tease me. (hahahaha I remember those days but I forgive you Ogo, Lele and Prince). And I thank my Mumma for being there to proofread, even if I ask her hundred times to review the same work, she never complained. Thank you always, Mumma.

A big thank you Chancellor Jack Hawkins, Mrs. Janice Hawkins and their daughter, Ms. Kelly for their huge support. To my professors for saying over and over again, Mac-Jane you are headed for greatness: Professor Rinehart,

Dr. Kline, Dr. Shannon, Dr. Harrington, Dr. Taylor, Dr. Davis, Ms. Bobbi Jo, Dr. Todhunter, Dr. Becky Ingram, Dr. Sun and Dr. Shelton. A big thank you to my uncle and his family (Prof. Sam Nwaneri) for loving and taking me in even though they just met me.

I am thankful to Mrs. AnniePearl Crayton, for reading my first book and believing in me.

Thank you Mrs. Lauren Cole for believing in me. For a great working environment, I say thank you to the people I met and worked with daily—Mr. Ivan, Mrs. Teresa Rodgers, Emily Reiss, Adrian Gee, Ratna Jain, Zeb Swindall, Ms. Ann and Mr. Kerry.

I am thankful for International Students Cultural Organization (ISCO), and the international office for giving me an opportunity to experience life with people from all over the world and walks of life. Thank you Mr. McCall and Ms. Silvia, Cesar Jauregui, Dean Darlene, Ms. Maria Frigge, Nyari Chanakira, Dr. Green.

I am thankful for my pastors: Pastor Messan and Aunty Angela Messan, Pastor and Mrs. Sola and Omowunmi Adewole, and Pastor Emeka and Chichi. A big thank you to RCCG International Worship Center, I am thankful for everyone who believed in my dreams. I cannot mention every name because of space but I say thank you. Thank you Mrs Wumi Abe (WumiMusik).

And to my friends, I say God bless you: Tobi Adegoke, Linet Nganga, Fadekemi Salami, Seun Okutubo, Seun Olubuyide, Yinka Bakare, MaryAnn Asuzu, Pastor Kay, Funlola Gaddis, Daniel Palama, Debola Oladaiye, Prosper Oladimeji, Morin Fifo and family, Seun Rachel Adunola, Anita Azu-Eni, Adeoye Adewole, Esther Ugorji, Bullen Timo, Andrew Mohandis, Marianna and Raza Razai, Jonathan Lockwood, Jim Eastman, Jamila Holmes, and Fred Yeboah.

God bless you all. I pray for you from my heart. Thank you for the support.

Love,
Mac-Jane

Chapter One

The morning was cold and as I lay on the cold floor shielding myself from the fierce angry weather, I longed strangely for the warmth of a body. Yes, I was young at heart but older than the Iroko tree in my Village. Today I feel strangely, the weather could add to it if you ask me. However, the situation of my body does not dictate my strength of character. Time and time again, Mamma had called me weather itself as no one fathoms my moods. Smiling to myself now, I pulled the blanket over my head and hugged my tiny bundle.

'Surprise!!!!!! Surprise!!!!!!' I heard Uneku scream my name from the next room.

'Please not now' I whined softly under the blanket.

'Surprise!!!!!!' Uneku yelled even louder.

Rising grudgingly, I folded the blanket and laid it beside my old 'Ghana-must-go' bag where my clothes belonged.

As I walked into the next room, one look at Uneku's face spelt trouble.

'Surprise, madam dey call you!'

'Where is she?' I asked, though I could have predicted very much that Madam Rose as we call her was in her room. She is probably sitting on her bed with her cell phone pressed to her ear, laughing in that funny loud manner she usually does while one of the girls busies herself painting Madam Rose's toenails Red. Taking in a deep breath, I tied the wrapper which was coming loose tightly around my chest and walked to Madam Rose's room.

'Madam say make u bring Orange, wey you go peel for her', Uneku stated in pidgin right behind me, picking her nose as I got to the door to Madam's room.

Hissing and rolling my eyes, I turned around and went to the kitchen to get some oranges and knife, wondering why Uneku waited till I got to Madam's door before she delivered her message. Sighing just one more time, I shook my head and felt the tears trying to find escape. I was tired of this life and longed for the warmth of my Father's house. Putting my sorrow away, I walked majestically into Madam's room with the Oranges in a fancy tray. And true to my prediction, Madam was on the phone and Tolu was painting her nails.

Laughing so loudly, I listened as Madam spoke at length with Alhaji Musa,

'Hahahaha!!! Alhaji, Alhaji, it is okay! Which of the girls would you like? Yes, yes, hahahaha!!! Ok Alhaji, I will send her over. Just the way you like them, young, lepa and pretty. Hahahaha! Okay Alhaji....see you later tonight....bye...'

Madam blew imaginary kisses to the phone and pressed the End call button. Dropping her cell phone on the bed beside her, Madam yelled at Tolu,

'You this good-for-nothing-girl, hurry up with painting my nails. Will it take you till Jesus returns to finish, eh?

'Sorry Madam', Tolu apologized.

'Madam, I have peeled the Oranges' I said.

Looking at me from my head to my toe with her large eyes to the point that I had to risk a peek at the large dressing mirror in her room to see if I had horns on my head, Madam collected the Oranges from me. Cutting one open, she sucked the fruit, extracting the juice and savoring the taste before she swallowed. Swallowing my own saliva, I looked away at the window and really prayed to be anywhere but here, in Madam's room.

'Why did you refuse Chief Odiegbu sex? Madam asked me

'Huh?' I scratched my head pretending I did not understand her question. Counting today my lucky day, I stared at Madam as she repeated her question.

'Since you don't understand English in the mornings, I will ask you again. Why did you refuse to have sex with Chief Odiegbu?'

'I....Because...em..because I am a Christian!', I stammered.

'Oh! So we are all going to hell right?' Madam asked upset.

'Will being a Christian feed you? Pay your bills? Will it... Will it??? Answer me!!!' She asked me, really shouting at the top of her voice.

I kept mute. I was young, and I did not fully understand what it meant to be a Christian but one thing I was certain about since the day I made the decision to follow Jesus, was that sex before marriage was wrong. So I made up my mind to remain a virgin.

'Look, you have to leave this house this minute and don't come back', Madam told me in that calm voice that meant 'just obey or disobey and get trouble, full version with no part two'.

'Yes Madam', I replied and started towards the other house to get my rickety almost nonexistent personal luggage. Cringing, I hugged myself in my mind's eye as I could still hear Madam cussing and swearing!

'Yeye girl... Stupid vagabond...silly fish', Madam Rose cussed.

Carrying my clothing in a green colored 'Ghana-must-go' bag I walked into the streets, with tears streaming down my small face, I longed to be in my father's house for the third time this morning. Sitting at a street corner, pulling my knees together to my chest, I cried some more. Why? I asked no one in particular as I stared without seeing into the harsh weather.

Wishing and willing my world to start again, from the time I was born, from the time I was papa's little princess, from the time I meant the universe to my brothers, from the time I sat on Papa's laps and ate fried snails.....Oh!! If only my life could start all over, I would not be here. I would be in Papa's big house enjoying being the favorite child.

Heaving regrettably, I remembered in a mighty rush of memories the last day I saw my beloved family, two years ago.

****

'...So help us God in Jesus' name!' Isaac prayed.

'Amen!!!' We chorused.

Papa, as we love to call our father loved to lead the prayers during family devotion. And this morning was not an exception as he started by asking Reuben to lead us in short choruses. After which we read the bible with Papa giving each of us an opportunity to explain what we understood from the passage. Today we read the book of Isaiah 11vs2-3 which says,

> *"The Lord's spirit will rest on him –*
> *a spirit that gives extraordinary wisdom,*
> *a spirit that provides the ability to execute plans,*
> *a spirit that produces absolute loyalty to the. Lord.*
> *will take delight in obeying the Lord.*
> *He will not judge by mere appearances,*
> *or make decisions on the basis of hearsay."*

Smiling really hard, I stared into Papa's face as he explained in detail what that bible verse was talking about. Papa's deep understanding of the scriptures marvels me and makes me desire a deep unending knowledge of God like Papa has. However, as much as I was so enthused about devotions, my brothers were never excited. In fact, they were always either half asleep through prayers or more than anxious to share the grace as Papa always ensured we shared the Grace, pointing a finger and saying it to a member of the family closest to you. And like every other day, my brothers mumbled the Grace and were just too anxious to go about their business. For the first time, I was anxious too for prayers to end, I had a dream last night which I wanted to share with my family.

'Papa'm I had a dream', I blurted out as Papa and my brothers set to get up from their seats.

'Was it a bad dream Nne?' Papa asked me.

'No Papa'm', I said, shaking my head quickly.

'Last night I dreamt that I was very big. I saw myself married, living in a beautiful big house with glass walls and crystals glittering. In the dream, I was a very important person as people answered me Yes Ma, Yes boss every now and then. I had a lot of male and female servants. Then, I saw you and my brothers come to me to beg for money...'

'Shut up your mouth', Papa rebuked, closing my mouth with his big palm.

'But why Papa?' I asked in the innocence of a child, confused.

'You must not repeat that dream again', Papa told me as I looked at him wide-eyed. I love Papa and I respect his opinions very much, in fact I have always looked forward to hearing Papa speak. But this counsel was beyond me, I just could not understand it. This was the same way Papa rebuked me and hushed the news of the first dream I had, I thought to myself as I remembered sadly how Papa called it 'Aru'. He felt it was an abomination for my elder brothers to beg money from me. Let alone, me, an ordinary female child be head over them.

'TufiaKwa!!' Papa said repeatedly as I relayed my dream that day.

Dusting their buttocks, my brothers got up and prepared for work. Peering at their faces, I felt the sneer but it could be just my imagination. Like Mamma always said,

'You fantasize too much, Somke! That's your problem, eh nwam!'

I have always thought Mamma to be too tender, just like the dove that descended on Jesus at His baptism at the Jordan River that Papa described at devotion one morning. So, in my child-like reasoning, I concluded that Mamma was too squashy (soft) to understand and believe in the passion of a born leader. Rising sadly, I looked in the general direction of the room, nodded at Papa who was flipping through the Guardian Newspaper and went to my room to get ready for school.

Chapter Two

I am always amused every time Mama told the story of my birth. She has told it several times, yet I never get weary of hearing it.

'Congratulations sir. Your wife has just delivered...'

'Oh Doctor, I hope it is not another boy?'

'Oh well sir, you should first of all thank God mother and child are okay before considering the sex of the child.'

'Oh Doctor, I know that but the fact is, if my wife just gave birth to another boy I am going to leave the house for them, gbam! Seriously, I am tired of having boys everywhere, full stop.'

Sighing, the doctor looked at the sad man who stood in front of him, with hands on hips the doctor lacked words to say. To the doctor, this life was a mystery. Some walk into the hospital hoping for a girl or boy while others come in crying for the doctor's help to conceive. But here is a man with eleven sons yet unhappy.

'Well this means then you won't be leaving the house for them because your wife has just been delivered of a beautiful bouncing baby girl'.

'Hey Doc, you don't say'. The excited man said in shock.

'Of course sir, you now have a daughter. Congratulations once again'.

'Ehhh... thank you Doctor O!' the excited man beamed with smiles.

'So finally, Mama Katunga has decided to give me a girl child, eh? May God be praised o!' danced the happy man. Singing to himself, he went into the ward to see for himself if he truly had a daughter in this life! Hahahahaha...

Standing at the door of ward, the man beaming with smiles stared at his wife as a nurse handed a tiny bundle of beauty encased in a fluffy pink blanket to the tired but content mother to breastfeed. The woman raising herself just a bit carried the baby, settling her between her bosoms looked into the baby's face and looked up to the heavens as if to say, "Lord I thank you for this child". Then she brought her breast and positioned the nipple into the baby's small mouth. The happy woman smiled as her baby took her first meal. Heaving a sigh of relief, she looked up and there standing at the door watching mother and child was her husband.

Immediately her smile ceased as a worried expression replaced her smiling face as her gaze fleeted between her child and her husband, she swiftly stole a glance at her child suckling contently on her arm and back to her husband.

'Mama Katunga, how are you?' the man asked.

'Emm... emm... I'm fine Dim', she replied unsure of how to respond.

"Ah! Thank you my wife for making me proud. Finally I can say that I have a daughter, my own princess, and my own Ada", the excited man beamed with smiles as he acknowledges that he has an 'Ada', which is a title is given first daughters.

'Yes oo! We thank God", the wife replied, content.

****

At the naming ceremony, tradition demands that other women and well-wishers dance behind the couple carrying gifts to give to the child. The procession danced forward and the baby was handed over to the village pastor. Truth be told Isaac was not happy that his precious and only daughter is to be christened by a mere village pastor but since he could not afford to make his wife unhappy after giving him a daughter, he granted her wish.

"Praise the lord" pastor Miracle said.

"Halleluyaaah!" the crowd chorused.

"The Lord is good" pastor Miracle said further.

"All the time", the crowd responded.

'Today we are here because of the great miracle the lord has done for our brother, Isaac and his family' pastor continued. Isaac reluctantly went through all the ceremony and could not wait for the naming to be over so that he can enjoy with his friends.

The pastor continuing, he explained the reason for the gathering and thanked God on behalf of the family for the blessing. Then whispering into the ears of Isaac he asked for the names of the child, whispering back Isaac told the pastor. Hesitating, Pastor Miracle looked at Isaac's wife, raising his eyebrow in surprise and Rachael nodded to confirm whatever her husband must have told the pastor.

Clearing his throat, the pastor announced the child's name.

"And she shall be called Somkenechi Surprise Isaac....."

And at that the crowd started laughing, murmuring and whispering to each other "what sort of name is Surprise?"

But the noise soon died down as the pastor cleared his throat and continued, however, not without chuckling at the name 'Surprise'. After naming the child in the name of the Father, Son and Holy Spirit, the pastor declared the ceremony open for item-seven which was a memorable part of any African ceremony because it is when food is provided and you can eat, drink and dance as much as you want.

And the child grew....in size and in strength.

****

"Mama!" Katunga called entering the kitchen.

'Hey, Katun, you are back'

"Yes mama".

"How was school?"

"Fine mama, our teacher said you must come and see her tomorrow".

"Oh yes, I almost forgot." Rachael responded using a big spoon to stir the food on fire.

"Katun, call Somke for me".

"Okay mama."

"Surprise mama is calling you", Katunga shouted. Shaking her head, Rachael wondered when her son will grow, kids still been kids, he shouted her name right from the kitchen instead of just going straight to where she was to call her. "Surprise!" Katunga shouted his sister's name again. The child who had just turned four was happy to know her big brother was back from school.

"Welcome dede" she greeted.

"I got you something" katunga said pulling out something from the back pocket of his khaki short.

"Really?" Eyes wide with anticipation, Surprise held out her hand to collect whatever katunga would have bought her.

"Uhm...take" katunga said placing small colored shells into her tiny palm.

"Oh! They are beautiful, dede" Surprise exclaimed staring at the shells in awe. Beaming with smile himself, she asked where their mother was, excited to show their mother her gift.

"Mama is in the kitchen"

"Yayy".

"Momma, you call me? Surprise said walking into the kitchen. Turning around, Rachael stared at her daughter and couldn't help but smile at the fond way she called "momma".

Chapter Three

'Momma! Momma!!!' I shouted Mama's name, almost running into her.

'Easy Child, eh', Mama said touching my shoulder as if she was dusting off dirt from my blouse.

'Sorry Momma', I apologized.

'Momma, see what Papa bought for me', I declared in excitement with a TV commercial kind of smile plastered across my face.

'Hmmmm, very beautiful', Mama said, examining the colorful patterned Jacket.

'Papa said he bought it from Obodo-Oyinbo just for me'

'Really? Hmmm, that means your Uncle Nkporo must be back from the white man's land', Mama explained.

'Ewo!' I exclaimed, clasping my hands over my mouth.

'Yes Nne. Come, we must cook his favorite meal quickly, he will surely visit tonight', Mama told me.

Uncle Nkporo is Papa's immediate younger brother, living in Germany. Papa have never been to Germany but talks about it well as though he has lived there all his life. Uncle Nkporo looks nothing like Papa but hearing each speak, you will know beyond any reasonable doubt that they are kin. Uncle Nkporo knows so much and speaks the exact way Papa talks, even in his gesticulations. In our village, Papa and Uncle Nkporo are the most respected of men but most people told their children to be like Uncle Nkporo. I was proud of him, and hoped to be like him one day. I wanted to live in the white man's land too. But, like Papa said, I can't until I am done with the University, graduating with an excellent grade.

'Momma, do you think I will come first this term again?' I asked Mama, suddenly wishing to be through with secondary school so that I can proceed to the University, where I can graduate quickly and visit the white man's land.

'Nne, just study hard, e nu?' Mama said to me.

'But Momma I need to know how I am faring in school. Remember this is our final term before the West African Examination?' I told Mama.

'Somke, I know. That is why I have just explained to you to study hard',

'Momma, I want to go to Obodo-Oyinbo', I stated while I looked down at the pepper I was grinding for Mama as if the answer to the quest in my heart lay there. Mama kept quiet, continuing to pluck the vegetables off their stock.

'Momma, I want to travel with Uncle Nkporo to the white man's land', I repeated as if Mama needed hearing aids to hear what I had said earlier.

Sighing deeply and without looking at me, Mama asked, 'To do what child?'

'I want to be rich like Uncle Nkporo', I told Mama.

'But traveling to Germany will not guarantee your wealth, child',

'It will Momma! I know, I can feel it', I insisted.

Dropping the vegetables Mama was cutting, she looked at me as though I had grown horns overnight. Then she shook her head and picked the vegetables up and continued her work.

'Momma, you are not saying anything', I touched Mama's hand to get her attention.

'Somkenechi, it is well o! Just read your books child. For Christ' sake you are only 16years old!' Mama said at last.

'But Momma...'

'No buts Somke, now finish grinding that pepper for me. I need to add it to the soup',

'Okay Momma', I agreed soberly and stared right into space, hoping against hope that I would figure this life out very soon.

'Mama!' Katunga, walking into the kitchen called to mama.

'Dede!!' I said in excitement. Ruffling my head, Katunga smiled at me and went over to tell Mama that Uncle Nkporo and Papa were in the sitting room.

'Dede, I have something to show you!', I told Katunga smiling from ear to ear.

'Ah ah Somke, let your brother rest before you bombard him, e nu?', Mama rebuked me.

'It's ok Mama', Katunga intervened on my behalf.

Glad, I grabbed Katunga's hand and pulled him to my room to show him the Jacket Papa got for me.

'Somke! Somke!' I heard Papa call my name.

'Yes Papa'm', I answered brushing off dust from my skirt and running to the sitting room.

'Good evening Uncle Nkporo', I greeted Uncle Nkporo and then Papa.

'How are you my dear? Wow! Look at you, you are a big girl now!' Uncle Nkporo said touching my shoulder and pulling me to himself for a hug. Smiling sheepishly, I looked at him and felt like an ant beside an elephant.

'I am fine Uncle Nkporo. How was your journey?', I asked even though I expected the usual 'cool' response in that funny ascent he uses, speaking as if he was speaking through his nose.

'Cool my Angel', Uncle Nkporo said and I smiled to myself.

Spending the whole evening at the feet of Papa as he and Uncle Nkporo exchanged stories till far into the night when Mama had to cajole us to bed, was an unforgettable experience. Oh Yes! Though sleepy, I enjoyed every bit of the evening, listening with rapt attention with dreamy eyes that stared far into the deep well of Papa and Uncle Nkporo's eyes.

****

Saturday mornings always bring the smell of freshness, especially after the chores have been done. Mama will serve us boiled yam with eggs fried in a manner Mama called scrambled, sounding almost like Uncle Nkporo when he says; 'scrambled eggs and toasted bread please!'. Breakfast on Saturdays is one day everyone looks forward to and today is not an exception as we all ate silently. Each hoping that the plate of yam and scrambled eggs would not finish. Sitting with my brothers listening as they told stories about work, we heard Mama cry out in sharp pain. Running as fast as our legs could take us we rushed to her side only to realize that Mama's water just broke. Ever since Mama got pregnant, everyone has been pampering her especially as she is took in after 16years since she had me. Papa is so afraid she might lose her life. A friend suggested that the doctors aborted the child but Mama says the baby is her miracle child. We are all so worried but we have to believe with Mama and be strong for her. After they had me, Mama never dreamt of ever having another child but here she is today heavy with another child, wishing with all her might that she had listened to the doctor and had gone ahead with family planning.

'Chim o!' Mama's scream in pain pierced right into my thoughts and brought me out of my reverie.

'Ndo Mama', my brothers chorused each trying to hold her and guide her to the hospital.

'Get her bag to the car', Reuben told Katunga

'I think we should call Papa', Katunga said.

'Ehhh! My waist o!' Mama screamed

Wide eyed, I looked as Mama writhed in pain while my brothers scampered about, seeking ways to comfort her and take her to the hospital. On getting to the hospital, Mama was put on a stretcher and wheeled to the theater. Yes, I was young but Mama insisted that I went into the labor room with her. Stepping into the theater holding Mama's hands, I looked around and I concluded within myself that there was nothing 'delivering room' about this place. If you asked me, it looked more like a slaughter house. Very likely, the colors, the instruments and Mama's groaning sounds have clouded my sense of judgment but then I did not care. I felt nauseous. I wanted to run away, far far away from this world where women were allowed to groan in pain if they must bring forth a baby. I wanted to scream for the nurses to stop, the doctors to make the pains go away and for the Pastors to intercede and pray to God Almighty to remove the labor pains from womanhood! Chai! I said aloud and realized that about twenty pairs of eyes had stopped all they were doing to look at me. Shaking my head, I touched Mama's forehead and whispered to her ears, ' Ndo Momma!'

'Ewo o!' Mama shouted. 'I want to poopoo o!' Mama said, grabbing her thigh. 'Eh! What is this o?'

'Momma, sorry', I said rubbing her back.

And by now the contractions had increased to three in ten minutes. Before I knew it I saw the Nurses hovering over Mama, the doctor came and they placed Mama's legs apart, hanging on a pole.

Then someone told Mama to push.

'Push! You can do it. Take a deep breath. Breath out', the Nurses and doctor encouraged Mama till we heard the scream of a baby and then a Nurse who stood beside Mama said to her, 'you made it Mama Katunga. Congratulations! It's a girl',

'Huh?' My ears tingled at that information. "Wow! I now have a sister". I felt strange at that news, I could not describe it. I was torn between jealousy and excitement. The prospect of having a sister was tantalizing yet I was envious of the little bundle knowing fully that I would no longer be pampered as the only girl and last child. However, my misery and mixed feeling was short lived as Papa came out from the doctor's office later that evening, a ghost of his former self. I wondered what could have gone wrong, but I did not think any further as the cute little princess was placed in my arms. I looked into her face and saw a tiny replica of Mama and I simply fell in love with my sister. Her eyes were wide, seeking, questioning and deeper than the oceans. They were so penetrating as if to say they were seeking to know the intents of your heart. Her lips were small but full, just like mine. I had to smile as I saw a piece of me in her body. My baby sister came that afternoon amidst joy and sorrow as Mama lost her life that evening. We could not believe it and I wondered for the umpteenth time, what went wrong. I thought the Nurse said Mama made it, how come she is no more? I cried. Heaving deeply, it dawned on me that the mantle had fallen on me to be a mother to Kate and my brothers.

Chapter Four

Life was not the same without Mama, Papa was cranky and moody most times. He stayed longer outside, sitting in front of the house and staring into space. He cried sometimes and even asked us one day if it was only him that death befell. He wondered if he was destined to be a widower and queried why his wives will die leaving him in this ugly world. I made up my mind to ensure Papa did not feel Mama's loss. I studied harder at school, took care of my brothers and Kate and even resolved not to go the white man's land anymore. I wanted to care for Papa in his old age and be his perfect little girl. This new me endeared me to Papa and he loved me even more. We became closer and he told me practically all that he should be discussing with my brothers. Unknown to me, a string of hatred had already begun to trickle into the hearts of my brothers and was building a big web of hatred within them. I noticed that they were hostile towards me and told me more than often to stop acting like their mother. I could not fathom the attitude but I attributed it to the huge loss and gap

Mama's death created amongst us. We all laughed less, joked less, ate in a hurry and even Katunga had stopped bringing me tidbit of gifts on his way from work. I missed Mama daily but I was glad I have Kate to care for. Kate grew daily and I sure took care of her. I ensured she was not stigmatized and pushed to the corner or being blamed for Mama's death. Though a chubby cute baby, she looked like Mama in every sense. Papa could not bring himself to look at her as he described her as 'eyiri Nneya', as he felt she was a true copy of Mama except for the lips.

It was a Monday morning and I had just finished bathing Kate, I fed her with the baby formula Papa bought and placed her on the bed to sleep. I put her between two big pillows to prevent her from falling if she rolls. Just when I thought my chore was over, I heard Papa call for me.

'Somke!'

'Yes Papa', I answered running to Papa's room.

'When you are done with your house chores, you will go the company and give your brothers this file', Papa told me as soon as I got to his side.

'Yes Papa, let me quickly bathe', I replied wiping my wet palms on my wrapper.

'O di Mma', Papa agreed.

Leaving Papa's room, I went straight to the bathroom after stealing a peep at Kate, to ensure she was still fast asleep. As I bathed, I sang quietly with excitement at the prospect of going to the company. I loved going to Papa's company where my brothers work for him, especially now that Mama is no more, Papa hardly visits the company. He does all his paper work from the house and has entrusted the running and management of the company to my brothers. Katunga and Reuben know so much about investments and property, so they saw to the overall management of Papa's company. I hoped one day my brothers will allocate an office to me and let me work with them, but then I worry as they say I'm only but a woman. They often ask me what I know about *Men's* job.

And cracking my tiny head, I wonder over and over again, what exactly a *man's* job entails. Hmmm....., life seemed unfair to me, especially womanhood especially if their interpretation means I'm not ever going to work in Papa's company.

Well, forcing my attention to the present, I wrapped the big pink towel around myself and stepped into the room. Creaming my body, I selected a simple black dress to wear. I brushed my hair, applied lip gloss and checked on Kate one more time before I headed out. She was still asleep, so I carried her to Papa's room. Kissing her cute baby face, I placed her in Papa's big mahogany bed and picked up the file from the table.

'Tell Katunga to call Mr. Johnson to reschedule my meeting with him, e nu?'

'Yes Papa'm', I answered, shifting my weight from one foot to the other.

'Hurry o! Before Kate wakes', Papa told me and I nodded my head knowing fully that Papa did not want to feed Kate when she wakes. Yes, Papa is still shaken by Mama's death but he was no longer withdrawn from Kate like the time when she was just born. Taking the file, I wore my color patterned jacket over the black dress I wore and headed for Cross Street, where Papa's company is situated.

****

'Good morning Mercy!' I greeted the receptionist on reaching Papa's company.

'Hey Somke! How are you?' Mercy responded with a huge smile plastered across her broad face.

'I am fine o!'

'Nice Jacket', Mercy said to me. Smiling from ear to ear, I told her a thank you which I felt was a bit too loud as people who sat at the reception turned to look at me, or was it the Jacket they stared at? Well, I'm not certain but I felt good all of a sudden and proud of my father's purchase.

Turning to Mercy, I requested to see my brothers.

'Oh! They are in the boardroom. They have a meeting now!' Mercy offered that piece of information.

'Oh! Really?' I replied not so surprised. In fact, I would have been more surprised if I had been told they were quite free. Knowing my brothers so well, they are workaholics; just like their father who has slowed down since Mama's demise.

'Will you like to wait for them?' Mercy asked me.

'Sure! I will wait.'

'So tell me, how's Kate doing?'

'Well, she's growing so fast! I was looking at her this morning and I couldn't believe how much she has grown. Honestly, I can't believe its 6months already', I said and then suddenly my eyes watered as I remembered Mama.

'Hmmm', Mercy sighed and said; 'it is well my dear'

'Yes I know. Thank you Mercy'

'Um, let me see if your brothers are through with their meeting now. Please have a seat Somke.'

'Okay! Thank you Mercy.'

Excusing herself politely, Mercy went ahead to attend to other clients or visitors while I went into Katunga's office to await my brothers.

****

On the other side of the block, on the 4th floor, boardroom.

11:45am

'Hey guys! Guess what?' Jerome busted into the Boardroom.

Stopping all they were doing, Katunga and the rest of the brothers turned to look at Jerome.

'What is that?' Reuben asked already getting irritated.

'The great dreamer is here!' Jerome sneered.

'So?' Reuben asked impatiently. 'Look Jerome, we have a lot of things to do today than spend our time discussing Father's little gossip!'

'But guys that's the point! I'm sure Papa sent her to check us out. Let's put an end to her and her dreams', Jerome stated as a matter of fact.

Shocked beyond the thought line, each brother stopped work and stared at Jerome for a good one minute. Finding their tongues at long last, each sought words to frame the state of his mind.

'Really?' Judah asked, confused.

'I don't understand', Katunga stated.

'See guys', Jerome started, pulling a seat and sitting. 'We complain daily of Somke's righteousness and holier than thou attitude. Why don't we just kill her, now we've got the chance?' Jerome finished with a devilish look in his eyes.

'But we can't kill her naaww!' Katunga wailed.

'But why not? Are you not tired of her reporting our every act to Papa?' Jerome asked but in the general direction of everyone.

'Yes, we are', Katunga answered for everyone. 'But we can't kill her, she is our sister!'

'Scheeeeew', Jerome hissed

'Sister indeed, yet all we ever did in Papa's eyes was wrong except for this company'.

'See guys, I need some space, so I concur with Jerome. Let's kill her!'

And at that everyone started talking at once, each for or against the motion. While it seemed sensible for their own gains yet it was indeed unthinkable for anyone's peace of mind. After a whole lot of hot argument, Katunga put an end to the dilemma.

'Alright guys, let's not kill her but we can hide her in a secret house. Let's kidnap her and keep her hostage in a faraway place where no one can rescue her', Katunga finished breathless.

'Okay, that makes sense', Judah said, a bit afraid of committing murder.

'So where do we find the house and shouldn't we do it outrightly?' devilish Jerome asked.

'Oh! That's not difficult guys. I know of a place out of town', Katunga explained, with the hope of rescuing Somke once everyone wasn't noticing.

'Humph! Okay o!' Reuben agreed.

So the brothers began to work out the logistics.

Then all of a sudden, the evil genius amongst them brought up another plan, which they all thought was a better idea.

'Hey guys, wait a minute. Why don't we sell her instead to be a slave for some poor farmer in faraway Congo or somewhere very remote?' Jerome suggested.

Continuing, he explained 'that way we can make some cash for ourselves and not be worried about staining our hands with blood'. Jerome smiled, feeling very brilliant.

Katunga and Judah were saddened but could do nothing about their brothers' decision.

And with that they contacted some mallams who gave them N300, 000 in exchange for their sister.

****

'Noooooooooo!!!!!!!' Isaac, Papa Somkenechi wailed.

'Ndo Papa', Reuben said to his father rubbing him gently on the shoulder.

'Why me? First my wives, now my daughter. What have I done Lord?' Isaac cried, asking no one in particular as he stared heavenward.

'We are sorry Papa, we've searched all the hospitals in the locality and she is not there', Judah volunteered.

'It's been three weeks now since my little girl disappeared! Who will bear my case? Who will?' Overwhelmed, Isaac cried.

Jerome led the procession home that afternoon after their escapade at their father's company three weeks earlier.

'Papa, on our way from work we saw an accident scene close to Cross Avenue, and we picked up this jacket. We are hoping it does not belong to Somke'. Jerome finished breathlessly.

Peering at the blood soaked dirtied colored patterned Jacket, Isaac hoped against hope that the jacket belonged to someone else, and not his darling daughter. Yet, he could feel the hunch that it belonged to his baby. This was the same jacket he bought for her. Oh no! He thought.

'Em Jerome, why don't you people ask around first? I want to believe it doesn't belong to Somke'.

'But Papa.....' Katunga started. Raising his palm up, Isaac stopped Katunga's explanation.

'It can't belong to Somke. I sent her to the company to give you people a document. Didn't you see her at the company?'

'No sir.' Katunga answered for the brothers.

'Eh! Well, let's hold on a bit, I am so sure she will come home once she can't find you at the company',

'Ok sir!', the brothers chorused even though they knew that their little sister was not coming home at all.

For days, they searched for Somkenechi when she did not return home that day.

Their experience at the police station was one that they would never forget in their life time.

Chapter Five

Putting my fly-away thoughts together, I locked it in the vault of my mind and concentrated on the pain of the present. Yes, I longed to be in my father's house, but I am tossed out of a warm house and right now snuggling in a street corner crying my heart out. I remember in bitterness that day at Papa's company when my brothers gave me out to that stranger who handed me over to Madam Ross. I could have found my way home, but I knew I was not wanted at my 'home'. My brothers sold me into slavery in broad day light and made it clear that I must disappear and never return home or they would kill me. Really, I could have gone back home, but what if they meant every word? I felt very bitter and concluded that I would never forgive my brothers for kicking me out of comfort. Yes, it is indeed a wicked world, I wailed.

Wiping my face with the back of my palm, I picked up my tiny luggage and started down the road to an unknown destination.

The air was cold and the wind blew in my face. I was hungry as my mumbling tummy reminded me that the angry worms in them would like to be fed. I walked on, ignoring the bites of hunger I experienced.

As I walked, I thought of what I could do. Lord direct my path, I prayed. Then like a cool breeze on my ear lobes, I heard the popular verse Momma always recited, '*.....when you pass through the waters, I will be with you; and when you pass through the rivers, they will not sweep over you. When you walk through the fire, you will not be burned; the flames will not set you ablaze*'

But Lord I am tired, I cried. This cold and hunger is worse than fire burning my skin I argued.

'*.......He makes me lie down in green pastures, He leads me beside quiet waters, and He restores my soul. He guides me in the path of righteousness....*'

And that part of the scripture Mamma recites caught my attention. I have never understood it like that and I wondered how this path I am treading now can ever be classified as righteous. Hmmm, I need food! I cried. I thought you said you would supply all my needs, I asked the Lord.

'Hey Surprise!!!!!!' I heard someone call my name. Turning to the sound of the voice I saw Unekwu. She was carrying a basket full of fruits. I believe Madam Ross sent her to the market.

'Unekwu!'

'Wetin happen Surprise? We have been looking for you....'

'Looking for me? But Madam sent me away. Were you not aware?' I asked Unekwu.

'Anyway, how you dey manage?', I looked away when Unekwu asked me that question as I could not afford to tell her that I had not eaten three days in a stretch now.

Picking two clean apples from her basket, Unekwu gave me to eat. Thanking her, I started to move on, when she unfolded her wrapper, dug her hand into her under pants and brought out a totally squeezed hundred Naira and handed it over to me. Overwhelmed, I thanked her profusely, though I feared for her that Madam Ross will cut her in two for her two pounds kindness to me, if she ever finds out.

'Eh en, Surprise e get one person I know wey dey look for house girl. You fit go work for am?' Unekwu asked me.

Shocked, I sputtered. 'Yes! Sure! Of course!!!'

Not believing my luck, I laughed like someone who was intoxicated with the kind of wine served at the wedding at Cana. Unekwu gave me the address of a house down east. Forgetting my hungry status, I just started off to the house, grateful to God that I bumped into Unekwu.

****

On getting to 2Illo crescent, I pressed the bell on the big mahogany door. A finely dressed elderly man came to the door.

'Good day lady. How may I help you?' I was asked. Surprised at his command of English, I stammered out the essence of my visit.

'Good day sir, Please I would like to see Monsieur Guillaume',

Perusing me like I was an old newspaper covered in dog's poop, he gestured with his left hand that I can step in.

'Wait here', he stated and walked into an inner room. After a while a young woman came to see, explaining in an accented English that she is Monsieur Guillaume's wife; the Madam. Impressed, I tried my best to impress her too. I needed the job.

"So have you done this kind of job before?" Madam Guillaume asked me.

"Yes madam. I can clean very well. And I am hardworking", I provided, hoping that it was all she needed to know to give me the job.

"Hmm that's *grand,* I mean big" she said, caught between speaking English and speaking French. I was amused, but how dare I smile about that.

"Do you speak English bien? Madam asked me, I nodded as I understood she needed to know if I spoke good English. And yes, I must thank Mama for always insisting I used my English tenses right. Humph, I miss Mama.

Anyway, after drilling me with more questions, Madam came to the conclusion that I was good enough for the job. I was elated. Ecstatic, actually!

Madam showed me around the house.

Chapter Six

'Surprise, I suppose my wife wants you to help her with the grocery. You can ask Mohammed to take you to Shoprite', Monsieur Guillaume told me.

I stayed in the house like I was part of the family. Most people who saw the way I was treated honestly thought I was the eldest child of the family. And surprisingly my French got better too. No one could believe how fast I picked up French as a third language. In fact Madame Guillaume called me a "natural" in her heavily accented French. I love been here, but trust me nothing compares to been in your own home. Whether I live here in plenty and comfort, fact remains that I am a slave in this town. That is reality. I do not belong to their family and I know one day I would wake up and things would change. One thing that keeps me going every day is the God that Momma always talked about. I miss Momma very much. I miss Kate too, and I know she must be a grown girl now. Hmmmm, life has a way of throwing hard unfair blows...

'Yes Oga', I said quickly getting out of my day dream.

Walking into the kitchen I picked the list from the kitchen cabinet and headed out to the garage. The Guillaums' loved me and because they thought I was different. According to Madame, they saw God in me. Whatever that meant, I concentrated on ensuring they saw that more often. If that's all it took to endear me to them, I better stay in check with that God.

On my way from the market, Cheryl the baby of the house ran up to me crying. Surprised, I picked her up,

'What is it Cher?' I asked the little girl hoping to get one of her baby responses of; 'Didier took my doll' or 'Didier won't play with me'. But got none of that.

Instead, wiping her eyes with the back of her palms she only said 'nothing', in the tiniest baby voice I have ever heard in my life.

"There has to be something making you cry, Cher. C'mon talk to me, what is wrong?" I insisted, knowing very well that Cheryl could not be crying in vain.

Wiping her eyes with the back of her back, she explained that her mother was leaving town for a conference in Ethiopia and would not let her come along.

"Oh I see", holding her to myself, I comforted her and explained how important the conference was to her Mom.

"But I want to go with ma mere", she replied in her sweet baby reasoning.

"It is adult stuff", I tried further to provide an explanation.

"What is adult stuff?" Cheryl asked in her childlike curiosity.

Sighing, I pulled Cheryl to myself and tickled her until she was rolling on the floor laughing.

And true to Cheryl's words, Madame Guillaume left for Ethiopia on Thursday. Putting me in charge of the house, she entrusted the running of the house to me.

Three weeks later the unbelievable happened.

"Surprise, has ma femme told you of our intention to leave this country", Monsieur asked me.

"Oh no sir", I shook my head and I was suddenly sad as the thought of leaving this family and searching for another job dawned on me.

"Oh oui, Surprise", Madame Guillaume chose that moment to walk into the kitchen.

"My meeting in Ethiopia was actually about a promotion we having been waiting for. And we are really happy that I--I mean, we got the promotion", Madame Guillaume finished, quiet excited.

"Oh wow! Congratulations madam... I mean, congratulations to the family.

"Merci. Merci Cherie."

"So when do you leave ma'am?"

"Em, we plan to leave as soon as everything is ready".

"Okay madam", I muttered, swallowing hard. I could not bring myself to believe that my good luck has ran out.

"I would help you get the children's things ready whenever you need me", I offered further.

"Sure. But that includes you too Cherie. You have been an amazing girl, learning French at such great speed and taking care of the house. We cannot ask for a better house manager. So I and my husband have decided to have you come with us."

Shocked, I just stood there with mouth agape. Reality setting in I ran with all my might, hugging and thanking the Guillaums' with all that is within me.

Lol... Ta da, I am going to the White man's land. Finally my dream is coming to pass.

For weeks we prepared for our relocation to the United States of America. Wow, I am going to America. I said aloud to myself for the thousandth time. Lol.

Sunday, 10:45pm

Murtala Mohammed Airport, Lagos, Nigeria.

"Hurry up Didier, don't leave your back pack there."

"Yes ma mere, gotcha."

Rolling her eyes, Madame grabbed Cheryl's doll off the floor and handed it to her. "Now you be careful with that doll Cher if you do not want to lose it on transit"

"What is on transit ma mere?" Exasperated, Madame looked at me for help.

Ruffling Cheryl's hair, I trudged her on towards the gate.

Being my first time on an airplane, I almost swallowed my tummy when the plane took off. I thought my world was crumbling and sitting at the first class wing did nothing to quell my fears. I held on to my seat so firmly for about an hour, till I was certain we were not about to die. For some reason which I could not understand Madam Guillaume found me amusing. She laughed so hard until I was embarrassed and let go of my seat. For fear of the unknown I slept throughout the flight. Only occasionally waking to go or take Cheryl to the Loo.

Arrival at the Montgomery Airport was nothing like I expected. The fresh December wind gushed in my face and no amount of jackets prepared me for the cold. The weather is nothing like Nigeria's, not even in the rainy season. Madame should have warned me to wear a blanket instead. Um, now that I think about it, I think she did. Well, not to wear a blanket actually but to keep warm as she said "s'il vous plait assurer que vous garder au chaud ma Cherie parceque je crois qu'il va y avoir du vent quand nous arrivons". Now I wish she had explained that we would be arriving in a freezer. Urrgh!

****

"Surprise?"

"Yes Cheryl? What is it?"

"I think I'm in love"

"Excuse me?" I blinked my eyes twice to be sure I was not asleep. We have barely lived in America for two years, now all hell is let lose. What can a five year old possibly know about love, huh?

"I said I think I am in love", Cheryl repeated with all seriousness.

"Um, okay. So who or what are in you in love with?" This is one of those moments when I wish I was not a nanny, what can a 19year old me possibly know about men, and

I have not even been lucky in that department. I have never had a boyfriend, and now a five year old is going to get one? I did not know if I should cry for myself or wish to be an innocent five year old in love. Maybe I can find love that way.

"A boy!" Cheryl confessed, in childlike excitement.

"Okay Honey, so tell me about him. We better start the story from the very beginning".

"His name is Williams and he is English. Ooh I love Englishmen", Cheryl giggled.

"You do?"

"Yessss!"

"So, Cheryl how do you know you are in love?"

"I know because my tummy flutters every time he walks into the class and just like ma mere always says, when it is love you know it is love"

"Wow! That's a lot of wisdom there."

Chuckling a bit, Cheryl shifted her weight from one foot to the other and gave that face I have come to know so well that means I want to cry.

"Oh no honey, what is it?"

"He doesn't love me back"

"Who?"

Rolling her eyes, Cheryl blurted "Williams of course!".

"Oh yeah. Sure. How do you know he doesn't love you?"

"He's never kind to me"

"Oh baby, I am sorry", I drew Cheryl to myself in a hug, wondering what on earth I am supposed to say to a five year old about *love*. It is not like I knew anything about love except for the million love novels I read and romance movies I never get tired of watching.

"Well, Cheryl dear life isn't always about boys. I am sure you would meet kind boys later in life. You are just five years old honey"

"I know Surprise. But my Sunday school teacher says 'love is a feeling that you feel when you are feeling a feeling you've never felt before'. And that's how I feel about Williams"

"Oh Cheryl!!" And that was all I could mutter. Hmmmm, who would think that I would be discussing love and boys with a five year old. And frankly, I had no experience in that department. Cleaning and vacuuming? Yes, I am an expert in that field but my resume on love and men is so blank. In fact I worry that I may never meet someone who would love me. Mm-hmmm...I wonder if I am ugly. Why can't I find a man? I cried inwardly.

Two weeks later, Cheryl comes home from school with a smug smile on her face. Her prince charming English boy Williams kissed her on the cheek at recess. Lol... Oh America! What won't we hear or see?

America was nothing like I imagined. Yes, nothing at all. I worked pretty hard and was glad madam enrolled me at the university. I still lived at home with the family and attended Alabama State University. It was a great experience. All of Momma's teachings did nothing to prepare me for life in a university. With all the American boys trying to get me on a date. And Ah! Halleluyah! I finally get to be noticed by guys. It is amusing how they try to mimic the way I speak."I want a cheese burger", with my heavy ascent so deep you cannot miss it.

For me, I almost bite my tongue trying to pronounce *international*. I always think they say *inanational* when Southern Americans say *international*. It is a fascinating experience to hear people say "y'all" instead of "you all", and "Aiit" in place of "alright". It cracks me up every time I hear a young person, especially the cops, say "yes ma'am". Well, like they say, if you can't beat the pack, you join the pack. Indeed, that is who I have become. A strange southerner. Unfortunately, my native 'igboness' has refused to disappear. So, no matter how much American or French I try to become, my Igbo mother tongue still gives me away as a foreigner.

Anyway, back in the Guillaume's home, I got pretty comfortable. Being in charge of everything in the house, I had no worries in the world. And in fact, sometimes I even imagined living here forever, I felt like I have found my life's calling-- maybe I was called to be a house manager. I was too comfortable, if you asked me. But then, I did not mind. I got all I needed and every other person in the house respected me. It was much more than I could ask of life. Then, one day trouble struck my already peaceful life memento.

It was past 9pm, Madam was not back from her meeting in Chicago. Her plane would arrive Montgomery Airport at 9:15PM. Usually, Monsieur Guillaume loves to pick his wife from the Airport. I did not think tonight was an exception. So, looking at the time and surprised that Monsieur Guillaume was still at the house, when he should be at the Montgomery Airport to pick up his '*femme*', I decided that he must have forgotten what time it was. Thinking it smart, I walked to his door with the intention to remind him that his running late. I rapped lightly on the door to the master bedroom.

"Oui? Come in", Monsieur Guillaume said.

"Um, Monsieur it is 9:05PM and Madam's flight is scheduled to arrive at 9:15PM. I guessed that you must've forgotten so I thought I would remind you" I finished, very professionally.

"Oh thank you Surprise. You see, that is why I love you. You are so efficient", Monsieur said and walked over to where I stood.

Smiling proudly to myself, I said thank you and politely made to excuse myself.

"Oh not so fast Surprise. Please would you come in for a second? I need to discuss something with you".

"Alright sir." Closing the door softly behind me, I stood in front of Monsieur Guillaume, ready to take orders. He probably needs his shoes polished before he heads to the airport. I knew how impeccable Monsieur Guillaume loves to look. I always chuckle every time I see him prepare for bed, because he prepares for sleep like he is going for a meeting. Except for the sleep clothes, one would actually be convinced he was headed out.

"See Surprise, what I have to tell you is very serious. And I want it to remain between us, okay?"

Straightening myself, I prepared to hear whatever Monsieur Guillaume has to say.

"Do you like this house?" Monsieur Guillaume asked me, and I wondered what he was getting at. Without thinking, I gave him a very satisfactory explanation, plus the why I love the house. Seemingly glad, he continued.

"I would like to buy you a house like this in any part of the world you would like."

Shocked, I could not believe my ear. It took every ounce of energy I possessed not to jump on this man, out of gratitude. In a split second, I imagined all the wonderful things I would do if I had a place of my own. I would bring Kate over and start afresh with my sister. I would-- uh uh, wait a minute. Is Monsieur about to fire me?

Comporting myself- body, mind and soul, I requested to know why he would rather have me in another house instead of helping Madam here in the house, which was why they hired me as a house manager in the first place.

"Sir, I really appreciate this kindness, but don't you think Madam would rather have me here in the house doing what I know how to do best?" I managed to ask in my most professional voice.

"Yes, I understand that quite well Surprise. But look, you are now a grown beautiful woman and I can give you anything you want from life only if you become my mistress."

"Your *mistress*?" Doubtful, I must have heard wrong I concluded within myself.

"Oui, my dear. I can buy you the world if that would make you happy. I could even ensure your family joins you here in America."

The mention of family brought fresh thoughts of Kate. Honestly, I almost gave in at that point. But then, how can I do this great evil against a woman who has been so good to me? I found favor in her eyes. She has put me in charge of everything in her household, except of course, her husband. How can I even think of sinning against that God Momma taught me about? How can I displease that God Momma taught me to pray to each night? Humph, life is hard. I thought.

"No sir, I ca---n't." I stammered out.

"Yes, you can and you will." Monsieur Guillaume insisted with such vehemence I have never seen before.

"No sir, I can't wrong Madam" I tried to explain.

"Who has asked you to wrong Madam? All I am saying is that if you refuse to give me your sweet ripened fruits freely, I'd take it by force. I will pop your cherry. I have watched you grow, under my wings you have blossomed. I nurtured you into this beautiful woman you have become and I very much intend to have a taste of you before others grab you. So you better cooperate and enjoy the benefits of been my mistress or I'd still have you, either way. The choice is yours, Cherie. Decide."

Determined not to give in, I decided to call his threats bluff and walk out on him. Just as I reached for the door knob, he grabbed me. In succinct terms, I told him to let go of my arm. Well, I believe I sounded more like a whimpering puppy as he paid no attention to me. Determined to fight with the last drop of my blood if it came to that, I tried to shrug his arm off me. Luckily, my jacket came off and I made a beeline for the door. Just as I made to turn the door knob, madam opened the door. Shocked. Ashamed. Afraid. I could not look at Madam.

"What is going on?" Madam asked.

"Can you imagine this little ungrateful mutt trying to seduce me? Monsieur Guillaume supplied.

I need not tell you what ensued after then. But I was lucky Madam did not send me off the house immediately and believe me, things were not the same ever again. I was not Madam's favorite anymore. In fact, one time Rosa the Chef, reported me to Madam that I stole the kitchen knife. And Madam believed her without investigating. Kitchen knife? C'mon, what would I be doing with a kitchen knife? Hmmm, whom may I plead my case to? I swallowed the mild maltreatment hook, line and sinker. After all, they brought me to America, I reasoned. The weeks went by slowly and harder. From weeks to months to years, Madam's attitude did not change towards me. Luckily, she still allowed me to go to school. Well, that she could not help as I was on a scholarship. I could not report my matter to the authorities because in all sincerity there was no evidence of my being maltreated. She never hit me but I could sense the hostility. And who would blame Madam? Who would trust a girl your husband claimed was trying to seduce him, with her jacket in your husband's hand? I did not think anyone would, anyway.

Chapter Seven

He grazed my earlobes, I cringed.

"Boss this is so wrong", I pleaded.

"Vien ici, you naughty girl!" Monsieur Guillaume commanded, pulling me firmly to himself.

So afraid of what I foresee was about to happen, I quickly sought an escape route from this entangling. I did not want a repeat of my Déjà vu experience with Madam Guillaume.

"S'ilvous plait Monsieur. For the sake of God, please stop". I pleaded again, hoping to touch his Christian conscious, after all, he claims to be a Christian. Aint it? I asked myself as Elmer, Debola and Dami would have put it in their bid to tease Esther, an ESL peer tutor. In other circumstances, I would have laughed and even joined in the joke in my newly acquired American ascent, "aint this man supposed to be a Christian?" But I did not laugh. The situation I found myself was not funny. I am yet to recover from his last escapade, no one still believes my innocence. I had avoided Monsieur Guillaume like a deadly plague, ensuring we were not in the same room together alone. Yet, I cannot explain how it is that I am alone with him at this time. Oh Lord! Could life be more unfair than it already is? Can't time and chance choose another to play its joke on? Why me? I wailed. But then I caught myself, who in this world deserves to be sexually violated anyway? Every woman reserves the right to freedom, freedom to choose to be sexually active or not, freedom to say No to forced intercourse, freedom to... Wait a minute, who is even listening to this ranting and preaching in my mind. My friend, Cham would have tagged me the modern mad woman of globalization and women emancipated group.

I felt monsieur Guillaume's grip tighten on me and got out of my historical raving and concentrated on getting far away from this devil in a man's body. Pushing with all my might, I pulled off his embrace. My jacket got turn in the process and I left everything in his hands and fled.

Monsieur Guillaume let out a scream, like a woman in labor. I cannot believe this man! I snorted. And then the whole household ran to his side. Whoa! Time and chance again. Couldn't you be more innovative in ordering my life? Now all of a sudden, the house is filled with people? Where were they all when I was pleading with Monsieur Guillaume to let go off me? Hmmm, where were they? I sobbed quietly in the room as I heard Monsieur Guillaume tell the world in a voice clear and loud enough to make Congress select him a presidential candidate, that he caught me sexually molesting Didier, and that when he apprehended me, I tried seducing him in other to prevent him from saying a word. Wait a minute, when did Didier come into the picture? Oh so now, the story is that I am sexually molesting a minor, a 12year old? Oh Lord! What could go more wrong in my already hurricane destroyed life? I sobbed harder.

****

In jail, I licked my wounds like a sore lonely dog. The state found me guilty of child molestation and I am serving my term. For some reason, the prison warder seemed to fall in love with me and I found great favor in her sight. In fact, in this time and age of Obama's administration where everything and anything is allowed, one jailer once yelled out that the Prison warder was my lesbian partner, explaining her love for me was because of our relationship. How people churn out these kinds of story amazes me. When she yelled out my supposed sexual status, I thought of my first experience with a young lady who was apparently confused about her sexuality. I sat by the pool, lost in thought as I stared without seeing at the sky. It was cold and I wondered for the umpteenth time what I was doing out in the cold. Was it really necessary for me to stay by the pool? Actually my interest was beyond the busy blue water, it had more to do with my fantasy which in my mind's eye was indeed magnificent.

Only if you could get a peep into my heart. Laughing out loud, I picked up the Francine Rivers' **Redeeming Love** I was reading and flipped to the page I stopped to continue reading

"Hey" someone said.

I pushed my glasses off my nose, looked up and saw this ravishing beautiful girl. I swallowed quickly, and swiftly reminded myself that I must not stare.

I smiled and muttered a "Hi".

"Do you mind?" she asked gesturing to an empty seat by my side.

"Of course, please sit ", I offered.

"My name's Lisa Lee", she introduced herself.

Before I knew it, we spent 3hours in the cold talking about sweet nothing. She was a very likable person and I liked her already. Somehow I enjoyed our chat and though it was cold none of us showed any sign of being uncomfortable especially with the harsh weather blowing abundantly on our faces.

Lisa Lee turned and stared at me intensely. I looked up and our eyes locked. For a moment I did not want to believe that look was directed at me, adjusting myself mentally I decided to give both of us the benefit of doubt so I pretended like I did not notice anything.

"What's your burst Size?" Lisa Lee asked me.

Surprised, I looked at her abruptly. "Excuse me?"

She whispered the question again and it dawned on me where the discussion was headed.

OMG!!

Did she think our little comfortable chit chat happened because I was gay? I thought about what could have triggered such, but could not find an answer.

On my bed that night, I reminisced about our discussion. I don't have to tell you what ensued between us but now it's pretty clear that there's some craziness in the air.

Now, my question is why would you look around you and decide you want to marry or date someone of the same sex as you? Please what's the bait? I asked a few of my friends the next day at school. But hearing a fellow prisoner call me a lesbian made me angry and I indeed felt I needed God to vindicate me. This labeling was becoming too much for me to bear. I have been called everything, child molester and now a lesbian partner to a prison warder? What???? Well, what can I do but pray to God to vindicate me? King David's prayer came to mind; *"Deliver my life from the sword, my precious life from the power of the dogs. Rescue from me from the mouth of the lions; save me from the horns of the wild oxen"*. I prayed that psalm like my life depended on it. Now, the days that I spent reading the psalms suddenly yielded good fruits. Who would have thought that someday I would be accused wrongly and put away in jail? Who would have thought that one day I would gladly recite the Psalms Momma ensured we read every Sunday morning? Who would have thought my only friend would be the bible?

"Oh! Oh Lord! Vindicate me", I prayed softly at the corner of my cell.

As I sat in the corner praying, I heard that the Pastor from the African Church in Montgomery was at the prison again. The Pastor was originally from Togo but he is the Pastor in charge of a church in Montgomery. It amazes me how he travels almost three hours every week to share the good news with us. Today, for some reason, I was very excited to see him. And I looked forward to the bible study time. He brought some one along with him today. A young lady. Hmmm, she looked about my age. I was surprised when he introduced her and said she was rounding off her Master's program in International Relations, at the Troy University. I was even more intrigued when she lifted up her voice in worship. I have never heard of anything like that, not even Momma's sonorous melodies at Saturday devotions compared to this encounter. She sang like she was God's personal worshipper, like she sang personally to God in other for His presence to come to earth. Hmmmm, I sighed. I longed for what she had. I desired to worship God like the way this young woman did. Interested to know how she did it, I wrote her name in the memory of my heart believing that one day I would be free, free from this jungle and I can ask her for secrets to true worship. I hoped. I prayed. I knew immediately she was somebody I must get to know. Concentrating on the Pastor's sermon, I listened as he encouraged all of us, and more importantly brought the message of the cross in a manner that made even the prisoner with a reprobate heart to repent, genuinely. I smiled, remembering Momma's days of rigorous bible studying and ensuring we all went to that "Yoruba Pastor's church", like my Father's sister would have put it.

At that moment I longed for freedom, deciding to visit the church in Montgomery. And if I had my way, surely, I would love to be a part of the worship center. The Pastor's words brought new thirst for God and I knew the Lord will vindicate me someday.

I looked around and saw as everything progressed, the jailers went about their business like President Obama paid them millions of dollars to watch over us. I chuckled. I did not blame them, because, even the other government sectors did their job with such enthusiasm I concluded that there must be something fascinating about serving people. Even those statesmen from Texas, North Carolina, and Nevada, all seem to fall in sync with the system of service. I admired the trend. And thought about what a huge privilege it would be serve too. Maybe, one day, I would be a part of congress.

I laughed, yet a nagging feeling inside of me told me to hold on to my dreams. Reflecting, my mind went back to the America of the earlier centuries.

It is amazing how Alabama Statesmen could be so nice, given that this was the same colony where racial segregation was on high. Who would have thought that the native Indies as they were popularly known, after been pushed-- rather, forcefully ejected from their lands by the then President, would forgive America and embrace every stranger. Including me, in my 'Nigerianess', in every sense of the word. No matter how much I try to speak the American ascent, my mother tongue belied my identity. I am Nigerian, through and through. This is not to say that I dislike the idea of my nationality, it is just that in this moment of despair, it might just be best to plead alien. You know, claiming to be from out of space, with no jurisdictional identity. That way, maybe, I would not have to deal with the law that throws people into jail.

Hmmm... Who would fight my case, I sobbed. Angry at myself for despairing, my heart took courage and I busted out in melodies to God. Yes, difficult to worship in a time like this, somehow I found strength to praise.

I looked over my shoulder and saw Sarah Smith and Greyhound Ruth. They both looked downcast.

"What is the problem ladies?" I asked, approaching.

"We had a dream and we cannot interpret them", Sarah offered.

"I really wonder what the dreams mean" Ruth pondered aloud.

"Oh! Tell me about the dreams", I volunteered, knowing fully that all interpretation belonged to God.

"Well, in my dream", Sarah began. "I saw that that was growing fat, it felt like the less I ate the more I grew."

"Well, that could mean that you would be restored soon, all that you have lost will be restored" Laughing out, I asked Sarah not to forget me when she got out the prison.

Seeing that I gave a positive interpretation for Sarah's dream, Ruth was encouraged and told me her dream too. While we sat there talking about dreams, I remembered this story I read from a blog while I was in Madam Guillaume's house. I had dreams while I was out of prison but now that I sit here, I wondered what the future held for me. Would I one day be able to see my brothers and be proud of my accomplishments? Would my brothers one day regret selling me off into slavery? I wondered. I thought about the story on the blog because the young woman had dreams too. The writer talks about her walk to freedom. Still remembering the story as clearly as a blue sky, I recounted it my mind, line by line, word for word;

"She reached out, pulled me down on my knees and unto her laps. The faint smell of Spring bathing soap hit my nostrils as I placed my head gently on her wrapper. I sniff and feel the soft sob racking her slim frame. The hot tears drop on my body warming up my very cold heart. I did not blink or even turn my face to look up at her. If I did, she would drag me into her little pity party and drown us all. Tears showed weakness and sometimes some people deserve to see all your strengths. Her small soft palms slowly massaged my bony shoulders and I visibly relaxed, letting the tension, stress, pain melt away. The pain that leaves my heart thudding like a slowly winding down bell. Anyway, I am now immuned to it. It no longer matters how much he hurt me. What I needed was a plan, an opportunity to make papa see the stuff I am made of.

Mama kept shaking her leg in that absent-minded way of hers and my head almost rolled off her laps. I jerked upwards immediately but her hand stopped me, firmly but gently pushing my head back down. My mama, my only true friend. Sometimes, I wonder what she thought of me. A child forsaken by the gods? Stubborn and untamable? At least that's what papa always says;

"She is too stubborn for her own good..."

But what does papa even understand about what is good for me. To my papa, girls are only as good as their 'ofe owerri' that is, our native soup and their child bearing ability. If he was god, women will not be allowed to walk on the same paths that men walked on, they would be covered from head to toe in black coveralls and never to be seen except when food is needed or the urge for sex overwhelms him. Even at that, a man like Papa will kill the urge before it makes him display affection at his wife. I shake my head as images of his huge dark frame fills my mind. I believe that shaking your heads rids it of ill thoughts, this time around however, it did not seem to be working. Images of Papa barking out commands to me and Ukachukwu, my elder sister did little to calm me down as I watched the movie replaying in my head.

That evening, I had sneaked out to study with Oneku and Chioma, my two best friends. Papa forbids studying after school. He believes women should practice their cooking skills or try to please their brothers in whatever way possible instead of studying. Six hours of school was enough for a girl-child, moreover, what is the point of the whole education when she will still end up in the kitchen? That is Papa's theory.

As for me, I want to be a doctor. The white coats intrigues me and the air of importance fills me with such longing. Sometimes, I imagine I am the minister of Health in Nigeria. If Papa could read my thoughts, I would have been long dead. His TufiaKwa would be loud enough to rouse amadiohia, the village god from the spirit world. 'Tufiakwa' was something he did with his fingers to signify he forbids a thing from happening. As if that really works any wonders. Anyway, as I was saying, we finished very late and as usual, I tried to sneak back into

I and Ukachukwu's room only to see papa sitting down on the veranda smoking cigarette and drinking dry gin. I stopped in my tracks and watched him a little. He was obviously very upset. Many thoughts raced through my mind as I thought of the best ways to end the nightmare when I saw Ukachukwu sitting on the bare floor beside him. Her fair skin shone in the moonlight and the painful threads poked out like horns on her head. My heart beat faster as I walked towards them. Papa watched me come closer and answered my greetings quietly. I could see the tear stains on Ukachukwu's face. Once I entered my room, I realized I had made a big mistake because I could hear Papa's heavy breathing behind me. I did not have time to scream before he began to pummel me. Mama and Ukachukwu watched the fiasco from a safe distance, terrified that he would add them to it if they said a word. After he was satisfied that he had taught me another good lesson, he walked away feeling like a king and Mama rushed to me sobbing her poor heart out. The fear of Papa is the beginning of wisdom though I was yet to get wise. The love for medicine drove me. Like a woman in love, medicine became my lover.

Now, it's been twenty years past, and my once strong and agile papa has become frail and weak. Needing constant care after I diagnosed him of diabetes. No thanks his habit of constantly eating 'eba', a traditionally made cassava flour meal. Mama is equally old but happy. I watch her chat animatedly with my son, her grandson and for a minute I close my eyes and say a silent prayer to God.

I thank Him for taking care of me when I ran away from the house and only mama knew where I was. I thank Him for blessing mama so she could send me some feeding money while I worked and studied at the University of Lagos. I thank him for letting me achieve my dream. And now, I am a practicing doctor and a women empowerment activist. Papa cannot believe it's still the same me when he hears me give speeches on the television. I see the shock and pride on his face. I smile to myself and wink at Mama who gave me a chance at independence.

It is amazing that I can sit back today and enjoy my profession, only because I chose to be free from the clutches of traditions and rural imprisonment. If I had honestly paid heed to Papa, I won't be a doctor today. So, to my God and western education I say thank you for freedom. Yes, freedom to life and education and not wasting my skills in the kitchen. Laughing out loud... What a world we live in!"

As I reminisced over that story, I wondered if the story of my life would one day change for the best, and remain that way permanently. Anyway, Ruth and Sarah were soon out of prison. And it happened just as the Lord gave me interpretation and Sarah did not remember me.

****

One day, I heard my name been called over the speaker. Wondering what it could be, I sat morosely at my cell expecting the worst to happen. But then what could be worse than being thrown in jail for a crime you did not commit? I asked no one in particular.

The jailer looked at the paper in her hand, looked at me and looked again to the paper she had, more like she was confused; a look of surprise, joy and sadness. How anyone could reflect all three emotions at the same time was something I did not understand. Calling my name slowly like it was new to her, she fumbled at unlocking my cell. I managed a smile, more like a confused half smile. I did not know why I smiled but I still smiled like I sensed my best was yet to come. Oh! That song, my best is yet to come rang me in my head. I wondered where I had heard the song. I searched my mind for I felt God was telling me. It was blank. I thought it was blank. But I knew what I felt-- my best was yet to come. Humph... Sighing I looked at the jailer for a clue. Nothing came to mind. She only concentrated on unlocking me. I thought they were professionals at this kind of thing, why did this jailer take forever to unlock me? I thought.

Later on that day, I sat with a lawyer and he explained to me that I have been offered a job. A job? I blinked thrice. I was certain there was some kind of mistake somewhere. Whoever heard of a prisoner been offered a job before? In this country for that matter, a foreign country to me! How did that happened, I asked like my Father's people would have been quick to ask. At that moment I remembered Papa's siblings, their favorite clause was the 'how' question.

Every time something happens, whether good or bad the first thing they ask is 'how'. It has always baffled me how the first question they always asked was 'how' especially if it is a good news, like they expected you not to experience goodness. I remember Momma telling me that when she gave birth to me and aunty Chizoba came to visit her at the hospital, that the first thing she asked wasn't how she was doing or at least saying congratulations, but 'how manage?' "Sister, how manage?" I laughed so hard every time Momma told that story. How do you ask a woman who just had a baby how she managed to birth a girl? Hilarious! Some culture and people that is. Anyway, pushing my mind to the present, I tried to concentrate on understanding what the lawyer was saying. This was indeed a story that was worth the 'how manage' clause. I blinked again. Speechless. I could not utter a word. Tears strung my eyes but refused to flow. My heart was heavy yet I did not cry. The lawyer sensed my state of my mind and just kept re-assuring me I was not dreaming. For a moment I was annoyed at him, how dare he sit there and tell me, I was wrongly accused and the state will see to it that I was well catered for? How dare he tell me all will be okay? Where was he when I was suffering and licking my wounds? Can the State repay me enough for all the years I have lost? What exactly is he talking about? I looked at him with plenty of questions on my mind and definitely enough petty words to say to him to last him a century, if he still lived, but no words came out. I just sat there, staring. He kept talking but I did not hear a word he said. All that mattered at that moment was that I was free, free at last. Free to walk the planet. Free to visit that church in Montgomery. Free to seek God-- hmmm that last thought struck me. I did not realize that my heart sought to know God this much. I did not realize until now that I wanted to know Him. I was thirsty, not for the natural water but for the unknown God. I did not understand my hunger but all I knew was that I needed to grasp this God. My heart hungered. My chest felt heavy. But in all of it, I was glad. Indeed...

Chapter Eight

Life out of prison was not the same. People avoided you like you were a plague once they hear you were once imprisoned. But one thing made me glad-- I was free to worship. Free to discover the Almighty. Anyway, my new job was intriguing, I worked like my life depended on it. I left no excuses. I was my personal slave driver. I worked like there was no tomorrow. Life took a new shape for me and I peddled gently, afraid of the unknown.

I sat one evening at my apartment in New York, looking out my room when the mail man arrived.

"Ms. Surprise?" the mail man said, having gotten comfortable calling me that. I cannot forget the shock on his face the first time he asked if my name was truly Surprise. I always smile, every time he hands my mail over to me. My roommate has always joked that one day the mail man would ask me out on a date all because he is clearly in love with my name already.

"It is just a matter of time before he will fall in love with the bearer of the name", Nyasha often said in her thick Kenyan accent. I always laughed, amused by her prediction of my life by merely the look people give when I get introduced as Surprise. Sometimes I toiled with the idea of being called by my African name, my Nigerian name. But then, would that not even bring more attention to me. Somkenechi! I mouthed my own name, imagining the look on the faces of non Africans, even non Nigerians as they try to call my native name. S.o.m.k.e.n.e.c.h.i, I pronounced it again and smiled to myself.

Looking at the mail in my hand, I just muttered "thanks Bill", in my acquired American accent. I looked at the address on the front of the mail, it was from the United Nations. My heart skipped several beats. I shuffled to the closest sofa to me. I prayed it was good news. I applied for a position with the United Nations, I hoped I get something decent. Opening the envelope, I skimmed the documents quickly. I almost jumped off the window. I got the job!!! Yippee, I squealed like a little girl. I danced. I knelt on the floor, with my both palms lifted heavenwards, I gave thanks. "Ah! Jehovah extra-do, I hail you ooo!!" I praised. Who would have thought that a common prisoner would rise so quickly, from prison to the palace? I asked no one in particular. Settling more comfortably into the sofa, I read the terms of the contract. All of a sudden, my face was engulfed in fear. I have been posted to Nigeria. The United Nations needed an indigene who could speak the three languages fluently-- Igbo, French and English. I almost choked on the words when I read that part of the terms and conditions. I felt like my good life was about to be upturned, like I was indeed some kind of bad medicine intended for destruction. I felt like a bad omen, something to be spat out. I remembered too quickly how Papa spat out the bitter leaf soup the first time I attempted to cook the indigenous "Ofe-Onugbo", the traditional bitter leaf soup. Momma had always made that and Papa loved it best after his favorite "Ofe-Owerri". After Momma's death, I tried to make some 'Ofe-Onugbo' for Papa. To make a good bitter leaf soup you must wash the bitter leaves thoroughly. In fact, you have to wash it with both hands like the traditional way of washing clothes, till the rinsing water turns white. Feeling proud of my accomplishment that evening, I served Papa his meal. Papa smiled briefly, washed his hands in the wash bowl, dug his hand into the simmering hot garriumsulphate which we called 'eba', smoothened it in his palm, molded it into a small ball and dipped it richly into the 'Ofe-Onugbo' and he spat it out as quickly as he had put it into his mouth. There was no slow motion to it. I did not wash the bitter leaf well, apparently.

Focusing on the mail in my hands, I shivered. I could not believe where I was sent-- no uprooted to; back to Nigeria. I wept. Fear of the unknown held me hostage. I became a prisoner to my emotions. I could not imagine facing my brothers again. My wicked brothers. Several emotions churned in me at the same time, confusing my already scattered organized thinking faculty. I ran my hands through my hair, disheveling it the more. I felt like breaking something. I wanted to throw something, I wanted to--to-- to--, I stammered out unsure of what I wanted. But I was quick to come to a conclusion, I did not want to meet my family yet. Period!! How can I face the people who put me through this misery? How?

Gathering my emotions, I tried to live life like it was normal, when life for me was far from being normal. I was still rereading the letter weeks after I had corresponded to the Agency that I would take up the job. Sometimes, I was torn between writing back to turn down the offer, at other times my reasonable side took charge and reminded me that it was exactly the kind of position I needed to climb the ladder of success in my career. This particular Saturday was no different from recent weekends for me. I lay lazily in bed, willing the clock to be slower than usual. Then I heard my phone beep. I covered my face with my pillows, hoping that will make the ringing phone stop. When the phone would not stop ringing, I finally picked it up and looked at the caller ID. It was Veena.

"What 'sup gurl? Are you going for tonight's game?"

"Huh? Game?"

"Yea, at the stadium"

"Oh! Veena I didn't plan on going anywhere today…"

Well, not to bore with the details of Veena's convincing speech, I threw on a short summer dress without a backward glance at my reflection in the mirror. Pouting, I tried very hard to laugh at Veena's jokes though all I really wanted was to go back to my bed or better still, go for a long quiet swim.

"Babe look at that! See…"

Veena shook me vigorously pointing in the direction of the footballers. Huh? I looked and then I went into a trance. Surely what or rather who I was looking at was heavenly. He was tall, slim (really slim- awkward for a guy), and really handsome. His beauty was beyond words, Surely God must have created him on a Sunday and he must have been born in November. He looked so pure, like heaven, almost divine. Definitely, this must be a god! I laughed out. I could not believe I had just drooled over a man.

Oh! Wow!! I let out softly.

Veena was still talking excitedly about the game when we bumped into Nazie, the only other Nigerian I knew since I came to the States. Nazie was calm, tall, handsome and very funny. We loved hanging around him. And even though Veena was a complete African American or an 'akata', as other Nigerians would have described her, she secretly professed undying love for this Nigerian man. I was always amused. Nazie was not my type, but we sort of liked each other like kin. Maybe, it is because we are both

Nigerians in a foreign land. He always introduced me to his friends as his sister. And he would not stop calling me, "Nwanem" in his unabashed Igbo accent. Every time he calls me his sister, I cringed. Not because I saw any harm in that, but more from I did not want Americans to misunderstand our relationship.

"Hey Nwanem, ke du?" Nazie asked, as he always did every time we saw. He spoke as much Igbo to me as possible, as if that would make it more pronounced that he is Nigerian. He did not have to. His heavy laden accent gave him away as a foreigner anyway.

"I'm good", I replied as usual.

"Hi Naz!!!" Veena quibbled, too excited to see Nazie. I smiled.

Going over to his side, she hugged him and I thought the hug lasted too long. But then, what is my own in the matter? She is a grown woman, after all.

Nazie talked a little about the game with Veena, before he turned to me and asked if I have heard anything from home. Home, being Nigeria. As usual, I shook my head. Only that this time, I felt guilty. I wanted to tell him I got a job with the United Nations and I have been posted to Nigeria. But then, I figured that would make the reality of the job more real. So I chose self denial.

We all visited a little more before Nazie invited me and Veena to his friend's party later that week. Naturally I did not want to go. But Veena would not want to go alone. So I agreed to go with her. Saying bye to Nazie, we started for the car park. As usual, Veena could not remember where she parked. So, we practically had to tour the parking lot to remember where she parked. Finally I remembered Veena parked in Gate C, and at that point I felt like giving myself a dirty slap for not remembering sooner.

****

Pssstt!!! The guys whistled, and I turned to see what was causing the raucous. She was indeed the image of true divinity.

The moment she walked in, I lost my senses. Everything that made me a man turned against me. I looked down and could not believe myself. My body was in full gear in anticipation of what is to come. Mm mm...What??? I muttered to myself. I must have her, I thought to myself.

All evening I could not concentrate as I sought ways to appease my evil insatiable desire. She was the exact kind of women I liked- fat, petite, round and full on all sides. Her body moved in such a manner that proved to me that she was ripe for plucking.

I looked for ways to lure her to a dark corner. She seemed oblivious to my interest, and that worked perfectly for me. In this game, I have learnt never to get associated by any means to targets. One must never leave any traceable tracks, all clues must be cleaned.

I watched her every move all evening. Then hugging her friends, she picked her bag and kissed one of the guys on the forehead. Hmmm, that seemed like the boyfriend, I thought. I pitied him too, as I chuckled at the thought of what is to come. Already, I could guess that he has not even had a taste of her. So much for being a virgin, I laughed wickedly. Ehhh! Bamboo on my mind, I said to myself and laughed.

I followed her out to the woods. She walked briskly, and I was amazed at her energy and strength as I supposed her to be easy to handle. She turned around abruptly, as if to say she felt her doom was close. I ducked behind a pine tree, she continued. I came out and called to her, she looked up and started running. I was surprised. I pursued, overtook her and dragged her deeper into the woods.

She screamed. She bit my arm, I cussed and gave her a dirty slap. She yelled. I held her mouth with my palm. I pinned her to the ground, grabbed her thighs and pushed the barrier to her innocence away. Thankfully, she wore a skirt. That surely made things easy for me. I did my business with her, and smiled with content as she writhed and cried on the cold dirty mud. I have had my fill, I told myself. I took out a stick of cigarette and lit it. She cried, moaned and I watched her. My good mother would have labeled me wicked, but who cares? She deserved what she got, I told myself as I always do every time I 'bamboo' a girl, as I tagged the devilish act of having brutal sex with unsuspecting women. This was easy, I sighed.

Removing the gloves I wore, I threw it into a disposable bag, removing every trace of me on her.

Poor thing, I spat out and walked off.

No one will ever find out. Catch me if you can...

****

I lay sprawled on that ground, crying my eyes out. In fact, I cried till I could not cry anymore. I could not believe what had just happened to me. I could not believe I had just being raped. "Ah!!!!!!" I yelled out in pain. In disgust, actually.

I cried some more. "Oh No!!!" I felt like my life was finished, I felt dead completely. At that moment, I remembered Veena and I wondered what had happened to her. She was supposed to follow behind me. I searched for my cell phone. Luckily, the battery still had life. I dialed Veena's number. She picked on the first ring. Apparently she has been sick worried about me.

The following weeks went pretty slow. I went from therapy to therapy, doing one police report to the other. The cops assured me my assaulter would be brought to the books. I hoped too. But I could not help the situation, I could remember nothing of the man who assaulted me.

Could my life get any worse? I sobbed. I hated the whole male folk. And my anger can be justified. They deserved my wrath. My spirit was bitter. First at my brothers, and now at this personal enemy. He is a complete pervert! That was all I kept muttering. I could not believe he violated me and took what belonged to me.

I cried even harder as if that could help stop my shivering. I was mad. That bastard took my virginity in cold harsh cruelty. I spat my poison at no one but at this rate, I felt ready to kill, ready to murder that beast for turning me into this animal. I became his worst nightmare. I thought of ways to revenge, to hurt him---no no no, to kill him utterly. I wanted to take the laws into my hands and just slaughter him like a ram meant for Salah festival. He was dead in my mind, as far as I was concerned. This was one of those moments when I willed cartooned characters to become real. I wanted to be superman or one of the X-men, so that I could swing by his house and roast him alive with my powers. Hmmmm... I sighed again.

Wiping my face I determined to make him pay dearly for hurting me this much. Him, and my brothers! I concluded. He, my brothers and the rest of the male folk had to pay for subjecting me to 18years of pain, of embarrassment, of shame, of suffering... 'They must pay dearly, every ounce of pain they caused me. They would pay!' I said, vehemently.

I declared war within. The war was on between me and the male folk. Every one of them. Tsk... I spat into the toilet bowl and twisted my fist. I flushed the toilet again, walked to the sink and washed my hands. I stared at my reflection in the mirror and I started to cry again.

'He took my virginity...' I continued to cry. I probably fell asleep on the bathroom floor, because I could not remember how long I had been in that position. I heard Veena calling my name. It sounded afar but when my head cleared I realized she was just outside my bathroom door.

"Surprise! Surprise!! Are you okay? Surprise??? Please say something gurl, are you alright?"

Rubbing my eyes, I sat up from the floor and looked at myself again in the mirror. I wanted to tell her I was okay, but I felt too weak. I was tired. My head hurt. I was dizzy and I felt like my world was draining out. Actually, the right word for how I felt was woozy but then LaElice once told me that there was no word in dictionary like that. I knew that, but it felt appropriate to describe how I felt. I told him that maybe one day it will have to be added to the dictionary to better explain when one feels dizzy, tired and whooped out at the same time.

"Yes, I'm aiit", I finally responded to Veena's questions.

Pushing the bathroom door open she rushed to my side and helped me to the bed. Handing me a glass of water, Veena watched as a mother hen watches her chicks as I gulped water from the cup absent mindedly. I looked out the window, and I knew at that instance that I was done in America. I made up my mind to go back home, to go back to Nigeria. At that moment I decided that the UN offer was heaven sent. I could not bear to face the world, this world that knew me and my story. First, I am ex-convict, now I am a rape victim. I have been labeled and I could not bring myself to be 'tagged'. I sought escape, and for me, Nigeria did it. I did not have to go to my village, I would live in Lagos. I negotiated with myself. I was not ready to face my brothers. I hoped, I believed that with time I will outgrow my emotions and live life like any other regular 28year old woman. With this resolution, I wiped my tears and looked forward to moving back.

Chapter Nine

Lagos was nothing like I remembered it. It smelled of sweat and fumes. I looked around one more time, taking in the scenery. I closed my eyes and opened it, hoping that when I opened my eyes things will revert to how I remembered my Lagos. This part of Nigeria was a city every one scrambled to live in. Yes, which I know. But never in all my knowing did I envision a Lagos, a city this crowded. I felt choked. And I felt like running back to Abuja.

When I first returned to Nigeria, I stayed in Abuja a couple of days to recuperate from jetlag and do most of the paper work with the United Nation's office in Abuja. Having being posted to my place of primary duty, I was excited at the prospect of working with street girls and homeless women. What better place to find them in clutter than Lagos, but then I did not think the heat and noise would overwhelm me.

Closing my eyes to the tale signs of weakness I concentrated on the task ahead. I had a meeting tomorrow on the Island. I did not have a car yet, I haven't even settled in yet. I still stayed in a hotel. I hope to start looking for a house next week though.

Amazed, I stood and looked out of the window. It is amazing how everybody is in a hurry in Lagos.

5AM, the next day I was already all dressed to be at Victoria Island.

Grateful to Governor Fashola, I sat in the BRT bus at 5:20am, on my way to the Island.

"Ole, ole!!!" I heard someone scream and people looked in the direction.

"Abeg give me my money, I no wan hear story o!" The one screaming thief said, holding on strong to the trousers of the other man.

I looked on as the story unfolded. People stopped to look at what transpires, before we knew it a small mob gathered.

"I go kill you for here o! You chop witch? Abeggimme my money", the angry man continued.

At that point, the traffic chose to move and my bus moved on. Pained, I looked out the window wishing I got to know the whole story. But who am I? A journalist? Not at all… Lol

Luckily, I got to the place of the office just in time. I spent the whole day there following procedure. There was just so much clumsiness at the project center. I could not believe that the same people we tried to help vehemently resisted help. I wondered at that attitude but concluded that it was simply a result of ignorance.

In my annoyance, I focused my energy on finding the next available bus home. Getting to the bus station, the long queue for BRT buses was discouraging. Checking my purse, I counted the change in it and contemplated taking a yellow cab home. I was too tired to stand much longer after standing all day under the sun, not to mention at how my tummy growled and announced to everyone who stood an inch to me that I was starved.

"Kai, me ne ne? I muttered. I did not where my Hausa came from.

I flagged a cab down and he called a ridiculous fare, aggravated I practically pursued the cab man off. Turning around I saw an approaching BRT bus, thanking my God, I started towards the bus. Despite the queue, mehn! You needed to see pushing. One man actually jumped through the window to get a seat, a woman was almost run over by people. Scared, I clutched my bag and just stared at the scramble. Hmmmm… I thought.

Who sent me to Lagos State? I asked no one in particular.

****

That weekend I decided to change my hair style, I wanted a new look. Naturally, I would have braided my hair myself. Living in the United States exposed me to skills I never knew I possessed, and high on my list was making my own hair, myself. But for some reason, I decided to go to the hair salon, moreover it was far cheaper than visiting a salon in Alabama. My first visit to the hair salon was very typical of my imagination.

"Ah! Madam, welcome o!"

"Thank you." I wondered why everyone called everyone 'madam' in Lagos.

"You wan make your hair?" In my mind I wanted to yell, 'of course'. Why would I be visiting a hair salon if I did not intend to get my hair done? Instead, I calmly responded by nodding my head and proceeded to show them the style I wanted from a picture on my cell phone.

Finishing my hair, I looked at my reflection in the mirror. I was not exactly satisfied but I was happy to have my hair done without having to worry about the cost of braiding. When she named her price, I automatically converted it to dollar and was glad again that I was back in Nigeria. In fact I gave almost fifty percent as tip and she practically kissed the ground thanking me. I was astonished at her profuse gratitude. I just smiled and merely raised my hands signifying it was nothing. Then I remembered my experience with my friends at David and Busters in US. It was a cool evening, Deoye was not working that day, Wole had just returned from the United Kingdom and Morin was back from New York, so we all concluded it was the best time to relax. Getting to David and Busters, we ordered food first. It was a great time, Nigeria had played against Bosnia and had won, so we all felt good and proud to be Nigerians. Faithful and loyal patriots! I laughed as I mocked myself and my friends at our minimal attempt at patriotism. We only claim Nigerian when the going is good. Proudly Nigerian, I scoffed. Anyway, relaxing after a good meal, Morin wouldn't shut up about LeBron and NBA. And boys being boys, Wole and Deoye indulged her. I watched on fascinated at Morin's expert knowledge on sports especially Basketball. Then one thing led to the other and Deoye and Morin struck up an argument about tips. Morin felt she would only tip heavily if the service was excellent, Deoye thought it more human and an act of kindness to give heavy tips because he logicalized that most waiters live off tips as they are usually of humble backgrounds. The waiter who had served that night was quite forgetful and mixed up our orders at least four times that night. So, Morin did not understand why Deoye would want to give anything other than the fifteen percent tip that the company recommends. She thought it extravagant on Deoye's part to squander hard earned cash on undeserving waiters. Deoye did not share her view but was quite adamant about giving as much as possible to waiters because they really need the extra cash. Well, I sat on the fence wondering about tips. Now, as this woman thanked me again as I headed out the door, I could only smile wondering what Morin or Deoye would say about how much I gave this woman.

Standing at the bus station, I hoped the BRT buses would come sooner. I did not want to stand much longer in the sun, I wanted to get home as soon as possible. Looking to the left and right, I contemplated flagging down a taxi but again I remembered my first experience from the Island. At that moment I made up my mind to buy a car. I waited this long, hoping I would be transferred back to the US, or at least to another African country. I had not contacted my family that I was back in Nigeria and I intended to keep it that way. I did not know if my father lived or not, but I was not ready to confront my brothers. I missed Kate and I hoped to see her some day but now was not just the time, I convinced myself. I was still thinking about what to do to get myself home when this couple on the other side of the road caught my attention.

I looked at the two of them. They struck me oddly as two people in love. The man looked old enough to be her father. He reminded me so much of an old cargo who finally made the 'doe', who sent message home and a wife was arranged for him. She was pretty, and looked smart. So she didn't look any bit like a village girl like I would have liked to describe her at best. But the man's potbelly and balding scalp left me wondering if indeed it was love in the air kind of business. Instead it brought memories of an article I read about this young lady's affair with Nelson Mandela. Yes, Nelson Mandela. When he died, a lot of people wrote, sang, and said different things about him. But one that got my attention was this article I read. At the time I thought it was a beautifully done piece. Chuckling, I wondered if I still felt the same way about the article. So I picked my phone and went straight to Google in search of that article. I figured that one more look at the article would douse my curiosity. My blasé attitude concerning things of the heart scare even me, sometimes.

"Yes!" I gasped, having found the article. Though this was not my first time reading this article, I read it like it was.

"With a smile to capture the heart of the unsuspecting blood like me, he swept me off my feet, with his charm and infectious smile. Though he is 95 years old, it feels like he's older than that. I feel like I've known him all my life. Technically, that's true. I've known him all my life. He's practically four times my age, yet I loved him. When I met him, I completely fell in love with his persona, achievements and the personal moments we shared.

I remember my mother's warnings to me about loving men old enough to be my father, worse even, in Nelson's case, he was old enough to be my grandfather. But then, I did not care. He had the influence and affluence in South Africa, he had the money and I could drive the best of Mercedes I wanted. I could live in Cape Town with the rest of the family, and enjoy the paparazzi that came with being a part of Nelson Mandela's life.

Now I look back at how he arrived at been this great, I do not regret our meeting. He completely changed the history of South Africa and forever, the world would remain grateful. South Africa and Apartheid; saved from the monster racial segregation... No wonder my research papers always end up having a line or two about South Africa and apartheid. Thank God for Nelson.

I'm sure you know I love you Nelson, but even more because of who you are: you are selfless. Staying in prison for almost half your life for the sake of others, running away from an arranged marriage to be with the one you love and making wise decisions to set South Africa on high pedestal as far as international politics is concerned. Yes, people may enthuse that you, the great Iroko tree has fallen but I am glad the Almighty created a being like you. For making a difference in the world, I celebrate your life and do not mourn your demise. Though it is all a dream that we had something special but I am glad I met you personally through the eyes of the world.

One lesson learnt from the life of Nelson, he made a difference in the world (for even the supposedly super power USA president to decide to visit South Africa to pay respects), when you leave this earth what impact would you have made on the world?"

Hmmmm.... I wondered on that question briefly. I wondered what the world would remember me for when I am no more. Suddenly I became sad. I felt like I would be remembered as a former prisoner and a rape victim. I did not want to be remembered like that. Heaving heavily, I tried not to remember my past experiences. Strength from nowhere engulfed me and I felt like righting every wrong in my life. But how do one right rape? Do I get my get innocence and virginity back? How do I wipe away from all records that I have never been convicted of a crime? How?? I almost cried but held myself. I was in public. But I sought escape. Seeking escape became something habitual for me. I always ran every time I remember my past. I sought escape like I mildly put it, as if that would change things. Gathering my things, I walked off in such hurry I did not see, in fact I did not even know where I was walking being that my initial priority before my run for solitude engulfed me, was finding a way home.

"Watch where you are going, lady", I felt a strong hold on my arm steadying me from falling.

"Sorry", I mumbled to the man I had bumped into.

"Are you okay?" Mr. Savior man asked me.

"Y-y-ee-sss", I stammered out.

I gazed into his eyes. It was an incredible moment. I felt the world stop and all I saw were those eyes, very penetrating and it spoke of untold warmth. I wanted to seek, devour the depth of his being but I caught myself.

"I'm sorry", I muttered. I did not realize he has been holding my arm asking if I was okay, indeed.

Who would be after looking into those wondrous eyes? But I kept my thoughts to myself though.

"Yes, I'm fine. Thank you. I'm sorry for bum..."

"Shhh... it's okay". He gave me a smile that stole my heart away completely.

I walked away from there feeling lost. Like I have just found something that belonged to me, yet that I could not have. The weeks after then turned into mid day fantasies. Sometimes I imagined he was standing right in front me, staring into my face. And today like any other day, I dreamt, imagined he was talking to me.

"Hello ma'am, I'm here to see the project coordinator."

I thought my eyes were playing tricks on me. I blinked thrice. I could not believe my eyes. Could I really be seeing him, my dream man, in my office?

"Excuse me? Excuse me ma'am?"

"Huh??"

"I said I'm here to see the..."

"Yea, I got that. I am the project coordinator. Please sit down. Gimme a minute, I'll be right back", I jumbled off my words and practically ran to the toilet.

Like fate would have it, Mr. charming eyes was indeed standing in my office, live and direct.

Calming my nerves, I went in to see what brought him into my arms again.

I later realized that Tokunbo was the financial advisor representing the firm sponsoring the present project I'm coordinating. So now, I have to work with Mr. gorgeous eyes. How anyone, especially me can concentrate at work, I wondered.

First we focused on work, but at the end of the project, Tokunbo could not hold back himself anymore as he pursued me and declared his love for me unashamedly. I contemplated playing a hard catch but I knew I would only be deceiving myself if I did that. So the moment he asked me to be his, I wholeheartedly gave in. I prayed that God will reveal Tokunbo to me. I did not pray to ask God if he was the one or not, but I figured that if God led me and revealed the true man that he is, I would know. My love for Toks grew, and by now I knew it was not just a fantasy.

I hated falling in love. It captured your soul, stole your heart, making you a prisoner in your own mind and body. The idea of love reminded me so much of Pastor Leke Johnson's sermon on love. He admonished singles to rather be in love than fall in love, his argument been that if you fall in love, you'd fall out of love someday. It sounded funny when he said it that day, and I laughed so hard. But now I understand better why being in love is different from falling in love. Love captures your totality. And indeed my love for Toks was no different, I was crazy about this dude and right now I was his prisoner at liberty. Hahahaha...

****

With Toks in my life, I settled comfortably into living in Lagos. I even contemplated turning down any transfers to other nations if the UN decided my time was up in Nigeria. Toks was my world and he made living fun. Just last week we visited the Obudu Cattle Ranch in Calabar. It was the best time of my life, not even the many wonderful places I visited in the United States compared to my excitement. Well, I willingly credited it to the presence of Toks in my life. Life was not just the same anymore, he was my American as I fondly called him. And today like every once in a while I sent a love note to his office to declare my undying life. A little bit old fashioned to mail a letter, especially in the face of Nigeria's postal service system but I did anyways. Coming over to my place later that evening, Toks tagged me as a hopeless romantic as he read my note again, aloud this time;

Toks was indeed the magic of my heart, the symphony of my music, the melody in my lyrics. He was my world, sun, rain and rainbow. He was an original. My American man. He was nothing like an African man, though African by blood. But he was every bit an American. He even smelled of America and nothing like the Lagos dust. Fresh, titillating and... and... and fresh.

Though we've had our challenges, but his voice was always cool, calm and soothing. Like the tender drops of the rain, it dropped on every leaf, tree, and house on a cool Sunday morning, constant, tender but clear.

Reminiscing over how I met Toks, my mind took a journey of its own into the past remembering my first crush. I waited at the airport for Madam Guillaume to arrive, with a magazine in hand when I noticed him. Again he coughed.

I looked at him from the side of my eyes. One glance at his basketball body frame and I knew I was in love. Pretending not to have noticed him, I quickly pulled my attention with full force back to the Magazine I was reading. I hoped and hoped he would at least say hi to me. My tummy churned at the mere thought of him by my side. I was lost in thought- no, in lust actually. I looked on at the Magazine without seeing a word. In fact, I had been on the same page since I sat across this dude who's bought my mind for the past 30minutes.

He wasn't exactly handsome, but he had a strange aura that attracted any woman to him. Well, not every woman exactly. But he sure, got me thinking. I like what I am seeing, that's all!

Like some kind of electrical force was at work, (or is it chemistry?) I saw him rise and walk up to me. Looking up, I stared right into his face as his tall frame stood in front of me, saying stuff I was certain made sense, yet I hadn't heard a word he said. All I could mutter was a Hi. Like seriously, a Hi? Come on, Surprise, you can do better! I admonished myself.

Aarrrgghhh!

Anyway, as Mr. mysteriously good looking kept talking, I kept admiring the glorious wonder of God's creativity. His nails were well trimmed, and I couldn't help but wonder how they would feel pressed against my face. On point, he put his hands in his pockets and I wondered if he read my thoughts. But then he asked me a question that brought me out of my day dream.

'Are you real or from the spirit world, little mermaid?'

'What??' I exclaimed. Whoever asks a lady if she is a water spirit in this time and age? And what's with the *little mermaid?'* name calling.

'Sorry I surprised you, I was just wondering about your beauty. Its different, it's not like what I am used to'. My prince charming offered an explanation for his query.

I was shocked but I was interestingly glad. He wasn't the regular guy, I was sure.

At that, I laughed, throwing my head back and showing him my perfect dentition and giving him that television commercial dazzling smile. Oh! I like what I am feeling. And before we knew it, we talked all night long, enjoying the serenity of each other's company.

Speaking of airports, I promised to pick up Tobi from the airport tomorrow morning. I and Tobi have grown to be sisters, only she wasn't from my tribe and definitely not any kin of mine. I met her in church, she was amongst the greeters who welcomed me at the entrance my first time worshipping there. She smiled at me as she said, "you are welcome sis, and God bless you". Indeed, we became sisters and I became a faithful member. I even attended Tuesday and Thursday services despite traffic on third mainland bridge on my way from work. I loved Tobi and I am forever grateful she welcomed me to church. I learnt more about God, and one sermon that struck a deep code in my heart was the worship as a lifestyle by Pastor Sola. Romans 12:1-2 gave me a better understanding that my life should be offered to God as a living sacrifice, that is, a sacrifice that is alive, my spiritual act of worship to God. Exclaiming 'my my my' like LaElice, I drank in that scripture like a sugary substance.

Anyway, getting to the airport, you won't believe who I met. Nazie!!! I never thought he would ever leave the US and visit Nigeria again.

Chapter Ten

I was excited to see Nazie again, live in Nigeria. Not because he called me 'Nwanem' but purely because we met in the US. Days ran into weeks and weeks into months, and he became indeed my brother from another mother. I could easily ask him to run errands I considered a male job and I enjoyed his undivided attention as his 'nwanne'. Toks was fine with the relationship and saw nothing amiss, in fact he and Toks spent most weekends when I worked at the Ikoyi club. He became a part of I and Toks lives. We invited him to all our outings and Nazie was introduced as my brother. Well, I figured that was what he meant to me and Toks, a brother, kin.

His sparked interest in Tobi was equally amazing as he labeled her 'that Yoruba girl' in his thick Igbo ascent. I always laughed every time he flirted with Tobi. I wouldn't stop teasing him about Veena. He told me I was not patriotic if I thought he would have ever married a non-Nigerian. I called him a racist for choosing not to marry

Veena because she was of another nationality. A lot of people would have jumped at the prospect of marrying an American woman and becoming an American citizen. That was not the case with Nazie, he professed unconditional love for Nigeria, and I wondered why. Not because I did not love my country but purely because I could not understand his concept of the idea of love. Here he was an Igbo man interested in a Yoruba girl, a girl not of his tribe yet he did not consider a man of his caliber marrying anyone who did not speak his mother tongue. I concluded that Nazie must be a confused young man, who knew nothing about love, tribe and nationality. I figured his professed undying love for Tobi was fake but I kept my thoughts to myself. I trusted my friend to handle him.

Hmmmm....like any other Saturday, I had cooked Egusi soup, the traditional Igbo soup and decided to give some to Nazie. Putting it in a white bowl, I rushed over to Maryland to drop it off at his place even if he was not home. I had a meeting in church and I did not want to be late. Calling Nazie, I told him that I was on my way to his place, he confirmed that he was home. Getting to his place was easy, I was glad the traffic was quite light. Rushing up the stairs, I rang the bell and could hardly wait for him to open the door. Rushing past him, I practically ran to his kitchen to put it in his refrigerator.

"Thank you Nwanne'm"

"No problem. I made it this morning and decided to bring some for you before hunger will kill you."

"Hahahahaha...you always know how to take care of me"

"Haba! It's nothing. So, I'll see you later. I'm going to church."

"You and church sef"

"Hahahahaha...abi ooo! It's all about God oo!"

He smiled slowly as he caressed my hand. Jerking back, I slapped his hand away.

"Kai Nazie"

The change in him was spontaneous. I did not see it coming as he lunged at me. His coarse hand reaching for my silk top. The scream I let out came from my soul as my heart droned in fear of the trauma of another rape. Then, the world practically went black.

****

"Ah!!!" I bit into my nails. I could not believe this was happening to me again. A Déjà vu? "Oh Lord! " I cried out. I wept. I wailed. I told myself I was inconsolable. It pained me even more because this animal was someone I called my friend, family. "Chai!"

This was indeed a tale of once beaten, twice shy. Only that this was not a wisdom pill I took, I bear the very evidence of man's wickedness and my own foolishness. I had lost in this case. I failed. I blamed myself. I trusted too easily, too quickly.

I cried myself to sleep most of the nights. And when I'm not sleeping I poked around the Internet reading up every jargon and information I could find on late menstrual cycle and rape. I wondered what I did wrong. I blamed myself for what I did not do. I should have slapped him harder. I should have called the cops. But even the thought of that made me nauseous. It was not like the Nigerian police would have done anything about it. For a moment I forgot I was back in Nigeria.

I became angry. A mad woman. I was raged. I felt helpless.

****

After the incident, Toks concluded we were going to be inseparable, to which I hated him. He called every chance he got, visited every minute he could spare and would not stop praying for me. He tried his best to encourage me but I hated his guts. I hated how he was so calm in my despair. I hated him for being consistent and saying in that soothing voice of his, 'it's going to be alright babe, let's just trust God'. Trust God? What for? My heart asked but I never worded it. Toks consistency and trust in God irritated me, after all he was not the one suffering, so it is easy for him to speak of us trusting in God. I bagged him with the rest of the male folk and constantly asked him what he wanted from me.

"Toks, I am finished, there is nothing of value in me anymore. So what exactly do you want from me?"

"Babe, I am not in this with you for anything. Love is unconditional"

"Oh please don't preach to me young man. I know the scriptures too"

Keeping mute, he just walked over to the kitchen to get me a glass of orange juice, he hoped that would calm me down. I hated orange juice, didn't he know that? Hmmpphh... I pouted.

I hated Toks for being so Christian. He tried to reach out to me but I turned away from him. He reached out again and I gave him that stare that meant that he needed to stay away from me. I just hated him for loving me. No-- I loathed him for loving me. Yet I hungered for his love, for his touch, for his unfailing understanding. How can anyone love someone as filthy as me? I wept. I loathed him more for loving me in my shame. I felt naked, uncovered. He saw all of me, the very depth of my embarrassment. I shivered. His concerned eyes flicked to my side. He removed his jacket and covered me. I wanted to throw the jacket off my body instead my body gave room for more quivering. I hated myself for being so weak. I felt like I had failed everyone. I cried with regrets at all the things I should have done to that monster in human clothing for turning me into this failure. I should have slapped him harder. I wept. Toks moved closer and wrapped his arm around me. Once again my fear and hatred for the male folk rose above what I could bear. I pulled away from

Toks. He tried again to comfort me, this time around I gave in, caving in to a volcanic wailing.

****

No one could should blame me for hating the whole male specie. For some reason, even my love for Toks seemed to dwindle. I remembered my cold nights on the streets of Lagos after Madam Ross sent me away from her house for refusing Chief Odiegbu sex. I felt bitter at God for letting me go through that if He knew I was going to violated eventually. What was the point of remaining a virgin if it came down to being raped at the end of the day? What was the point of chastity if not just once but twice have I been violated? What was the point of Christianity if God couldn't save His own? What did I do wrong to deserve this unkindness? I wailed.

I thought the scriptures said that the plans of God for us was of a future and an expected end? Isn't that what Jeremiah 3:10 declared? So, how in the heavens is rape, prison, betrayal any form of hope and future for a young woman who haven't wronged the world? Was it my fault that I came to this world?

I was bitter, angry at God for disappointing me. I felt that He failed. He should have protected me, but He didn't. I was tired. I felt weak. I was ready to die, I had given up on life. What was there to live for anyway...?

Chapter Eleven

I was tired of fighting God. It was not easy but I felt God nudging me to let go, to forgive those who trespass against me. Really? How do I forgive those who have wronged me for no just cause? Forgive my brothers? Monsieur Guillaume? The faceless guy that raped me at a party? Nazie? Even my mother? If she hadn't died, all these wouldn't have happened, I reasoned.

As I sat on my sofa watching the Disney channel, I looked on at the television without seeing. I was tired of life. I considered suicide. Moreover a lot of people do it, even famous actor Robin Williams was said to have committed suicide. If I killed myself, then what? Would it make the problem disappear? I was too young for this heart ache Lord, please if you are indeed there make this pain go away. I prayed.

I willed myself to sleep, but sleep was far from coming. I turned off the television and walked to my bedroom. I checked my emails and wished the torrent of emails from work to stop pouring. I felt my work mocked me. Here I was, a social worker attending to the needs of street girls, especially those who have been raped yet I am today a victim. Ha!! I bit into my nails. Life was so unfair. Clamping my laptop down, I walked to my bed and lay there.

Humph... I sighed.

I remembered all the good memories in Papa's house as a child. I remembered eating fried snails off Papa's hands. I remembered when Katunga brought home that tortoise. I remembered so many things. How did my life deteriorate to this low life point? How?

As I lay on my bed staring at the ceiling and wishing my life to be over, my phone beeped. It was a call from Toks. Not now Toks, I thought as I declined his call. The phone beeped again. I did not bother to check the caller, I was certain it was Toks anyway. Rolling over in bed, I covered my ears with my pillows. I heard the door bell go off. Who again? Can't the world just leave me in peace, I cried. I ignored the door chime, I was in no mood for visitors anyway. And it was not like I expected anyone. Hugging the pillows, I wished the door chime to cease. But whoever was at the door wouldn't give up. Then I could hear the banging on my door. Really? Don't people get it when you don't answer the door? Ready to yell my misery out at whoever was banging at my door, I got off my bed with a vehemence to murder, if it came to that.

"Yes??? Don't you understand leave me alone???" I yelled out as I opened the door before whoever was at the door had a chance to say a word.

"Somkene!" the visitor spoke so softly I stopped midway into banging the door on his face.

"Katunga?" the shock on my face at the realization that my brother was indeed standing in front of me paralyzed every sense of reasoning in me. His tall frame and Momma's features on his manly frame belied his identity. There was no way I couldn't have recognized him. He looked just like a male version of Momma. I could have recognized him a thousand miles away. Moreover, no one calls me Somkene the way he does. Hot tears stunk my eyes.

"Katunga??" I asked again even when I was more certain than life that he was my brother.

When he nodded in the affirmative, emotions I couldn't explain surfaced. I just stood there. I was torn between hugging him and pushing him away. I wanted to find out about Papa and everything. I thought of Kate, the joy of seeing my sister again hit me. I wanted to know why they sold me. But then I was overcame by my grief. I was angry, sad, no---angry, mad at what they have turned me into. I shut the door in his face.

"Surprise honey pleaase open the door. I'm here for you." I heard Toks say. Not until then did I realize he was there all along, and Katunga was not alone. How had I missed him? Now that explains the phone calls earlier. I sat sprawled on the floor weeping.

"Go away", I returned.

"Please honey, open the door. I can explain"

"Go away Toks. And take that traitor with you"

I was upset with Toks even more, not because he has wronged me personally but because he had brought the traitor to my house. How dare he? Whose side is he on anyway?

"Get out of my house!!!!" I screamed at the closed door.

I knew Toks had my best interest at heart but my mind analyzed otherwise. I could not bring myself to trust that he was on my side of the camp. After all, he was male too.

Tokunbo had ranted nonstop for a couple of months now about finding my family. He appealed to me relentlessly to look for them since I was back in Nigeria. But how could I face the people who have caused me misery? It was not a difficult task to find them. Papa's business had blossomed and my brothers were in the Newspapers every now and then. Moreover, Facebook made it even easier to search them out. I toiled with the idea of traveling over the rivers to see them, yet my pride, bitterness and unforgiving heart held me rooted in Lagos. Who wouldn't do the same? I rationalized.

So, I was not surprised to know that Toks had found my brothers. My shock was that he was at my door! And at this low point of my life, Toks decided to humiliate me further and drag them into my already shattered life! I did not think I could forgive Toks for this error. How dare he?! Why was Toks always trying to play God in my life? I wept.

I heard hushed voices outside the door and heard footsteps. I guessed they had gone away. As I listen for the footsteps, I sobbed.

Then more like an afterthought, I heard Toks say aloud from outside the door; "I'm sorry babe. I'm here for you if you need me. I will call you later."

For some reason, those simple words made me cry even harder.

****

For days, Toks tried to reach me. I wouldn't see anyone. Even Tobi. I was mad at the world. I felt the world was mocking me. I didn'twant to see the sunlight again. I wished the long nights to last forever, yet even the elements mocked me as morning came faster than I had wished. God never answers my prayers, I whined. Why worship this God that allowed hurt? The Almighty became my enemy too. I sat in front of the TV eating cheerios. I didn't even add milk to my bowl of cheerios. I was angry at the cheerios for not tasting the way I wanted it to taste. So I got up and poured it away in the trash can. I went back to the TV, coiled up on the sofa and I thought of ways to enjoy my misery. Suicide had never been an option for me. As a Christian I was taught not to take your life; that our lives belonged to our maker. But the growing child inside of me made committing suicide palatable. It saddened me that the child growing in me did not belong to my honey bunny, Toks never ever even kissed me!

Ah! I cried. Enjoying my self-pity and dwelling in my personal sympathy party I continued to lament on all the evils that have happened to me in this life. My phone beeped, it was a message from Toks still pleading with me to talk to him. How do I explain to him that I was pregnant for a rapist? I couldn't face Toks, so I ignored him.

****

Two days later, Toks bangs on my door refusing to let go until I opened the door. Having sold my heart to the devil, my heart was hardened. But after several hours of Toks persistency, I opened the door.

"Yes?" I asked with raised eyebrow.

"Surprise Somkenechi" Toks called my full name as if that explained why he refused to go until I opened up.

Standing there looking at him, my eyes burned with irritation. Why was he just standing there and calling my name, my full name for that matter. No one had called me Somkenechi since... since...

I remembered Katunga's visit and became angrier.

"Please leave my house right now!"

"Babe would you listen to me at least?"

Just go away Toks, I don't want to see anybody"

"I know babe, but I'm sorry about everything that has happened"

Annoyed, I almost screamed off his head. How does he know how I am feeling, what is he sorry about, huh?

"Sorry about what exactly Toks? Were you the one that got raped, not once but twice? Were you the one that was sold into slavery? Were you thrown into jail for a crime you did not commit? Were you? Answer me Toks, what exactly are you sorry about?"

Shaken by my outburst, Toks just stood there speechless.

"Yeah, that's what I thought. You know nothing!" I vomited, satisfied.

"Um...ERM..."

"Huh? Cat got your tongue?" I mocked.

"Stop your sarcasm Surprise, I'm not the enemy. I'm your friend babe"

"Yeah, right! Wait till you hear the latest development about me before you declare that we are still friends".

"What are you talking about?"

"I'm pregnant Toks!"

"Y--you're what?"

"Yes I'm pregnant Toks."

The reality of my announcement hit him like a heavy volcanic tornado on a cold Monday night. I saw fear flash across his face as he sank onto the floor with his face in his palm. Was he crying? I couldn't tell.

I felt sorry for him, though I was the one in the predicament. I knew exactly why Toks wept. His dreams of me as his bride just got shattered. Who could blame him? Now I'd be single for the rest of my life, that's if I even live to have that life.

Picking up his car keys, Toks just walked away.

Unlike other days, I did not cry. There were no tears left to shed. Awkwardly, I smiled.

For days I longed to hear from Toks but no word came. Not even a text message. I put myself in his shoes, who would want to marry someone in my circumstances. My phone beeped and it was Tobi. Picking the call reluctantly, I spoke into the receiver.

"Hey"

"How are you Surprise?"

"I'm fine. What's up?

"Um, I was wondering if you would like to take a walk with me and get some sunshine into your system..."

"Thanks Tobi, but I don't want to go out"

"I understand dear, but it's important you come out sometimes. You can't hide forever Surprise."

"Hmmm...."

"Come on gurl, I'll walk by your side all the way, okay?

"Alright " I grumbled. I heard her scream for joy.

"Oh my! I'll be there in a sec"

And yes yes, she was there in a second. Apparently she made the phone call from her car, outside my apartment. As much I hated to admit it, walking with Tobi did me a whole lot of good.

"So, have you heard from Toks yet?"

"Nope!"

"Hmmm...."

"Yup"

****

The pain was unbearable this time. I felt like my waist will cut in half. I held my waist and paced from one end of my room to the other. I wasn't sure what to make of the pain. It felt strangely like MP, you know we women always had a name for all the troubles that we face. I remember Tobi always called her lingerie ingredients and Esther once asked if I was killing fowl implying that I was on my menstrual cycle. I usually laugh at these ironic names used to talk about women things and issues but the thought of MP...or rather menstrual pain did not settle well with me, especially knowing my status, instead I continued to pace. I wished one of my brothers were here so I could ask him tostand on my back. But the thought of my brothers only aggravated my condition and reminded me of my predicament. Now that I think of it, why am I even analyzing the case of MP? I mentally had to remind myself that I was pregnant. Pregnant women don't have MPs, or do they?

I rushed to the toilet. Pulling down my shorts, I screamed in joy at the very evidence of my freedom.

I screamed, I screamed, I screamed!

Whether the baby was aborted or not, I could not explain but I was happy. I could not believe that I would one day be excited about menstruating. Hahahahaha...

I was not sure if I miscarried or if God finally heard my prayer, yet I was glad to see the blood stains that signified my womanhood, again.

To clarify things I decided to visit the hospital. On getting to the hospital, the necessary tests were performed. As I sat at the doctor's office awaiting the verdict, I pulled constantly at my painted fingernails in such great anxiety.

"I'm sorry Ms. Surprise, but our test results show that you never were pregnant. How did you get to the conclusion that you were pregnant?"

"Huh, doctor?"

"Yes, you were not pregnant"

"But doctor, I didn't see my menses that month after I was raped."

"Yes, I understand that. I'm sorry that you had to go through that. But it is medically proven that some women don't see their menstrual cycle every month, and stress and anxiety sometimes can prevent the natural outflow of blood"

"Really?"

"Yes ma'am. Did you do any tests to confirm you were pregnant after the incident?"

"No doctor, I just assumed once I did not see my menses at the next cycle."

"Woah. I see. A lot of women make this same mistake but I'm certain you know better now."

"Yes I do. Thank you doctor".

Leaving the doctor's office that evening, I felt two things. I felt like the happiest woman in the world and the most foolish woman on earth. At twenty-seven, one would think I have the genetics of the woman figured out. And to think I gave myself and others so much stress over this. Not to mention that it almost cost me my relationship.

OMG! Toks!

Picking up my cell phone I called Toks.

"I'm not pregnant Toks" I muttered into the receiver.

"What?"

"I said I was not pregnant. I mean I was..."

"Heeyyyy, slow down babe. I can't understand you."

"I'm sorry Toks, I'm just excited. Um, I'll be at your place shortly".

When I told Toks all the doctor said, he hugged me like his life depended on that hug.

Chapter Twelve

The days that followed my discovery brought mixed feelings for me. Sometimes, I was very excited about it and at other times I considered suicide. But with constant fellowship and study of the word of God, I no longer felt like dying, instead I took my job even more seriously, catering to street girls especially those that have been raped. Also, I sought justice for them, even though the police were not really 'your friend', I would not stop reaching every high power in government to ensure perpetrators were brought to book. Though I forgave Nazie, it did not stop me from turning him over to the Judge. He had to pay for his sins anyway. I figured that if I only forgave him, forgot about the incident and he walked away scot free then the whole point of me advocating justice would be lost, as many others like him would ask for forgiveness too and be loose on the streets to do more harm to other unsuspecting women. Moreover, the problems his singular selfish act had cost me cannot be justified. The law on him was not enough. Because of him and the other idiot in the US, I have come to hate sex. Hmmm... I sighed.

The idea of sex disgusted me. I was so appalled by the thought or even the mere mention of the word, that I considered puking. I lost interest in it and it no longer made sense to me. I wondered why God put the strong desire in man, and even animals. I pictured myself sprawled on our honeymoon bed, filing my nails while Toks busied himself on my body-- I concluded I would only allow him because the scripture said not to deny each other sexual satisfaction as man and wife. But trust me when I say, I have lost the slightest interest in the matter. I looked at Toks across the kitchen counter and I felt sorry for him. If only he knew...

I finally took Toks suggestion and visited home. My first happiness was seeing Kate grow into a fine woman. She was indeed a spit replica of Momma. I looked into her eyes, those eyes that I stared into the first time she was put in my arms. I wept as I remembered how Momma left this world. At least I was glad she did not have go through the agony of not knowing if I lived or if I was dead when I was sold by my brothers. As I saw Papa and Kate, I was overwhelmed. Pope Alexander's to err is human and to forgive is divine quote ran in my head. King Solomon's words in Proverbs 17:9 *"Love prospers when a fault is forgiven, but dwelling on it separates close friends"* also struck my heart and at that point I did not care what it took to forgive but I was ready to forgive. I cried. I begged God for strength to forgive my brothers.

"...forgive us our trespasses as we forgive those who trespass against us"

I remembered that part of the scripture, it is funny to think that Jesus knew that people will always wrong you but what was more important was to forgive no matter what. I knew it was easier said than done because I have been there and forgiving was not an easy task but I made up my mind to try. I forgave. I prayed earnestly to forget too.

Looking at Kate and my many little nieces and nephews, I just fell in love again with my family. Papa was old and I was grateful to God for letting me see him again. At least he would be able to walk me down the aisle and give me away to Toks in holy matrimony. Hahahahaha. I laughed. The idea of being married to Toks made me shy, even when I knew that no one could read my thoughts.

I sat there moping with mixed feelings --joy at seeing my family again, and sadness at what I had to go through to get here. I was indeed my Father's girlfriend, I was the woman on the side, sometimes never accepted by society, scorned and shamed by the world but still loved by Him. It doesn't matter what the world thought of me, I felt safe knowing I was in a relationship with the one who owned the World. I wanted to be His personal lover, His best friend. I was at peace as I made Christ my love and I became His girlfriend, all because I forgave. It felt strange to say I'm in love with Christ as Jonathan Butler sang but I must confess that I was more than ready to go through life again if it pleased Christ, and if it all happened so that my brothers would know him. But one lesson I learned pretty well was that God sometimes lets us go through the hard core of life to get us to our place of blessing. Life taught me that our suffering could be just for one soul to be blessed. I realized at that point as I looked at my brothers without anger or bitterness that if I died that night my job on earth was done. I smiled as I discovered the feeling of fulfillment in that singular knowledge. Oh! How heaven will rejoice that all my brothers are born again all because I forgave. Hmmm... If only I knew what my Father in heaven was preparing me for, then I wouldn't have grumbled. Like Pastor Mo' had once told me, precept upon precept, line upon line. But I was too eager to reach the future I did not allow God. Now, I'm so ready to let God, and follow His leading every step of the way...

Precept upon precept...

Line upon line...

Isaiah 28:13...

Words from the Author

'*My Father's Girlfriend*' was inspired by the story of Joseph in the bible. As I read through his experiences, I thought I could relate with his sufferings—rising from prison to the palace. Many women face diverse challenges globally, I thought that through this beautiful piece of work I can highlight on the need to say 'NO' to any form of female abuse and violence.

While you read this book you would find a lot of Nigerian terms and words. I wanted to present my world to you. If you are not Nigerian, this book gives you an insight of our society. This is not to say every part of Nigeria is filled with female slavery, but I believe the concept is a general phenomenon that affects the world at large. So, I hope you enjoy learning some Nigerian names, food and even our 'famous pidgin English', which is an informal way of speaking the English language.

Disfruté…

About the Author

Mac-Jane Chukwu is from the famous city of Lagos, Nigeria. She loves to learn and has been teased for not taking time to have fun; but that is not true and she is indeed a bundle of talents. She is the author of Open Secret and is currently working on another book. Having obtained her bachelor's degree in international relations, she is now pursuing her master's in this field with a dream of specializing in national security affairs; she hopes to create change in Nigeria and the rest of the world especially through international conflict management expertise. With her background in media production, Mac-Jane is equally interested in building people, hence her involvement in projects that encourage positive change. She is the executive vice president of the International Student Cultural Organization (ISCO), currently the graduate administrative assistant with the career services at Troy University, and founder of Tower of Hope Teaclub, a foundation to help troubled street girls. Like Joseph in the Bible, Mac-Jane wears a coat of many colors!